THE WINEMAKER'S SEDUCTION

Bank executive Madeline Watson never allows any man too close. Five years after being jilted she is content with her life as it is. Her mantra: No dating. No commitments. Never. No spending the entire night in the arms of a man—No. Never again.

Billionaire Sicilian chick magnet Giorgio Lombardo, ruggedly handsome, virile winemaker loves his carefree life. Jetting off on his private plane to inspect his vineyards, or driving through the Mediterranean countryside in his Lamborghini. Women drop at his feet—until Madeline Watson walks into it.

The uptight bank exec rocks his world, disrupting his carefree existence. Giorgio is happy to satisfy her craving for an un committed just *benefits* relationship. Giorgio finds himself wanting more. Now he has to convince the sexy blonde beauty to commit to him.

Can he convince her that he's her happily ever after?

THE WINEMAKER'S SEDUCTION

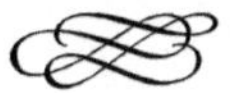

CINDY REDDING

For my Family and Friends, in this crazy year we all need a little escape.

CHAPTER 1

*M*adeline Watson was used to dealing with overbearing men. They generally thought the world revolved around them, and the sun rose in the sky just for their pleasure. Well, she would make Mr. Lombardo see how she could turn this inconvenience of having to go to him in Sicily to her advantage.

A bell tone chimed, and the fasten seat belt sign lit up. The captain began, "Ladies and gentlemen, we're cleared for landing and will be arriving shortly. Please remain seated until we come to a full stop. Thank you."

Maddie adjusted the belt and glanced out the window. She heard the landing gear lowering into place and peered out her window as the flaps adjusted. The plane banked slightly to the left as it made its approach over the aqua-blue water of the Mediterranean.

She'd turned her focus from loss mitigation at her father's bank, Watson Financial, to finance, five years ago, during the darkest point in her life. Fluent in Japanese, she had packed up her belongings, closed her Malibu Beach condo, and moved to Tokyo. After her father's medical scare, she moved back to LA. She was home for a month when her brother Michael, the bank's acting president, asked—no—told her she would have to meet with Mr. Lombardo. There wasn't any time for her to learn Italian, and she wanted this deal to be over with before she would need to say more than *Ciao*.

Maddie looked out the window. The water wasn't as deep a blue as the Pacific but just as beautiful. The Mediterranean's crystal-clear, aqua water was dotted with sailboats and colorful fishing boats, the hulls reflecting their shadows on the seabed. She was amazed at the sight from the plane. Unlike most landings she had been through, this one was over the sea. The plane began to land, and the water quickly turned to the tarmac of the runway. With a slight bump, the wheels touched the ground and landed in Palermo. Many of the passengers applauded and shouted, *"Bravissimo."* She glanced around at her fellow passengers, thinking, *Okay, that's different.*

Maddie got her carryon, the only luggage she had brought, and debarked with the rest of the passengers. Walking from the tarmac into the coolness of the terminal, she scanned the mass of people standing behind the waist-high metal gate, looking for her driver. No one held a sign with her name on it. "Oh boy, now what?" she mumbled under her breath.

Maddie walked through the crowded terminal, heading toward the line of taxis parked outside, hoping to find someone who spoke English, when a man came toward her.

"Madeline Watson?" he said. His deep voice held a slight accent.

She looked up at the tall, impeccably dressed man in a navy-blue suit. She couldn't help but notice how handsome he was. His dark, almost black hair was combed to the side, a thick lock falling over his forehead. His aqua eyes held a hint of gold in their depths. His tie matched the aqua of his eyes exactly.

"Are you Madeline Watson?" he said before his full, sculpted lips turned up at the corners.

The smile dazzled her. "Yes, I am. Thank God you speak English. How wonderful."

"I'm Gio—"

She interrupted, "I know you're my driver. I wish to go directly to my hotel. I'm exhausted and then later this afternoon…" she glanced down at her gold wristwatch, "perhaps around two, you can drive me to Mr. Lombardo's office. I understand that you were informed of my schedule."

Maddie rolled her designer carryon past him through the throng of passengers. Some craned their necks looking for friends and family, waving and shouting greetings. She walked toward the exit, the sign written in both Italian and English. His long-fingered hand reached for the handle of her suitcase as he said, "Allow me—"

"Thanks. But I can wheel my own bag." She inhaled a whiff of his cologne—spicy, and *very* sexy.

His smile broadened to show even, white teeth transforming his face, making him more handsome. If that were possible. "Ms. Watson, allow me to introduce myself. I am Giorgio Lombardo."

She blinked and felt her cheeks redden.

Giorgio had arrived late to the airport. He'd scanned the crowd of passengers who'd debarked from the flight from Rome. His gaze stopped on a beautiful blonde. Although petite wasn't his usual style, she caught his attention, then a smile tugged at his mouth. Was she the American bank executive he searched the crowd for? Her blonde hair fell in waves down her back, past her shoulders. She wore a dark-gray suit jacket, buttoned at the waist, that defined her hourglass curves. The straight-leg pants she wore hugged her pert bottom before stopping at her ankles. Black, red-sole stiletto heels completed the outfit. Ms. Watson rolled her French designer suitcase with authority, carrying the matching designer bag over one shoulder. Her beauty took Giorgio's breath away. Her perfume, a clean, fresh scent with a hint of jasmine, lingered.

Maddie, by far, was the most beautiful woman he'd ever seen. And that said a lot because Giorgio did more than look. Her moss-green eyes, the blonde of her hair, kissed by the sun, not platinum, but golden and wheat, her peach-stained lips, beckoned to him for a taste. What would those lips feel like as they parted? Her blonde, silky hair tented around his abdomen as she took him into the heat of her mouth.

"I have a better plan," Giorgio heard himself say. "Stay at my villa. You can rest, and then we will be able to discuss the Napa vineyard at our leisure."

One beautifully arched brow rose at that for a moment, then she said, "You have internet? Maybe Wi-fi, a printer, and a scanner?"

"At my home?"

She nodded.

"Of course, I do. This is Sicily, not a hole in the wall."

A delicate blush pinked her cheeks. "I'm sorry. I didn't mean to imply—"

He ignored the throb in his groin and raised his hand. "No, please don't worry. You'll have all the comforts of home and an office. Significantly better than the business center the hotel provides."

She smiled at that. "Thank you, Mr. Lombardo. That sounds great."

"My father," he put both his hands over his heart, "God

rest his soul, was Mr. Lombardo." He dropped his hands to his sides and flashed another smile at her. "Call me Giorgio. Okay?"

"As you wish."

They walked out of the terminal into the beautiful, early-morning, Sicilian sunshine. It was late September, and the weather wasn't overly hot. August's drought had almost been forgotten. Though that was the reason for the hasty harvest, and why he'd not been able to fly to LA to negotiate the purchase of the Napa Valley vineyard. They took a few steps to the curb, where Giorgio stopped directly in front of his matte-black Lamborghini. The roof was down, showing the red interior.

"Here we are. May I take your bag?"

"One minute, please." Maddie crouched down and unzipped the front compartment of her small suitcase and pulled out a hat, unfolding it to reveal a wide brim. "Thank you," she said, handing the bag over to Giorgio. Then she adjusted the hat on her head.

Giorgio opened the car door for Maddie, she slid in, and he closed her door. Then he walked around to the front of the car and put her small case into the trunk. *She didn't bring much.* He watched as Maddie sank into the red-leather seat, audibly sighing.

"It must have been a long trip for you," he said as he reached for his sunglasses.

"I hadn't realized… I did get some sleep on the flight from LA to Rome. My PA booked business class, and that worked out well. I did have a nice meal, and this morning, they served rolls and coffee. The amenity kit was perfect—" She raised her left hand, and he noticed that she had no rings on her fingers but a pretty pink nail polish as she covered a yawn.

"Sorry, I must be tired. Here I am talking about an amenity kit."

He chuckled at that and listened to Maddie's sexy voice as he drove through the heavy morning traffic on the outskirts of Palermo. Giorgio didn't bother to mention he had his own private jet. A gift he got from his Uncle Giuseppe DiMarco when Lombardo Wines expanded. She could have slept in a queen-size bed on his plane—If he gave her a chance to sleep, that is.

Gradually, the number of cars thinned, and the scenery changed from a mix of modern and old city buildings to palm-tree-lined narrow streets as Giorgio drove. He made small talk, something he never did as he navigated the cobblestone streets, pointing out some of the many sights. The scenery changed again as Giorgio steered the Lamborghini to the right and drove up a road with a low stone wall. They continued up the winding road, going around scissor-sharp turns. He occasionally tooted the car horn before going around a curve. Shifting gears, Giorgio slowed the car as they approached a large, intricately designed, wrought-iron gate. He reached one long, tanned finger to press a button on the console in his car, and the antique gates parted to allow them passage onto a gravel road lined with towering cypress trees. Ahead was a clearing as Giorgio drove up a hill.

Maddie said, "This is beautiful. What a magnificent view you have here."

A vineyard with rows and rows of grapevines spread over rolling hills. People were working in the fields; truck beds were full of straw baskets overflowing with dark-purple grapes. A large stone structure stood near the edge.

Giorgio said, "We call that the barrel room."

Then he pointed to the right, showing Maddie an olive grove. "I never get tired of this view. The oil harvest is usually in October, and we produce a nutty, robust olive oil. I'm not needed for that the way it was necessary for me to be here for the grape harvest."

In the distance, the Mediterranean acted as the perfect backdrop. And framing all this were two homes, both large, but one was a sprawling single story. He drove to the left but pointed to the right. "That home in the distance belongs to my cousin Ricardo DiMarco. And this," they arrived at a long, cobblestone driveway lined with cypress trees, "is… my home."

Maddie leaned slightly forward in the leather bucket seat. "This is your home?"

The grounds leading to his villa were dotted with palm trees in clusters of three. Between them were ripe lemon and some orange trees scattered along both sides of the driveway. The emerald-green, manicured lawn looked as if it were painted. Two towering palm trees stood among shorter ones at the end of the drive just before the circular entry began.

Maddie gazed up at the Baroque-style villa; the center structure was three stories high and, on either side, two-story-high wings jutted out. The entire structure was made of stone. Across the center of the main building, the second and third floors had French doors that opened onto balconies with wrought-iron balustrades. The first floor and the two wings had floor-to-ceiling French windows with wooden shutters. Part of the center was covered in climbing vines of bougainvillea in shades of blue and raspberry.

Giorgio came around and opened her door, then reached into the trunk for her suitcase. They walked on the cobblestone drive around a gurgling fountain to the main entrance.

Maddie's parents lived in Beverly Hills, but she'd never seen anything so beautiful as his home. A phrase, *old-world charm,* came to mind. "You live here alone?"

"You'll have privacy," he said as he opened the leaded glass door for her to enter. Maddie heard the clicking of heels running across the marble floor.

"*O signore Lombardo, si qui.*"

A petite woman who looked to be in her fifties with an olive complexion and short, brown hair stopped when she saw Maddie.

Giorgio said, "*Si, Maria, un momento.*" He turned to Maddie. "This is my housekeeper Maria. Unfortunately, she doesn't speak a word of English."

Giorgio spoke to Maria in rapid Italian. Then with a broad smile on her round, leathered face, she nodded toward Maddie and said, "*Scuzi, scuzi.*" Turning, she left the entry.

Giorgio gestured toward the ornate, curving staircase. A fresco of an ancient Roman ruin was painted on the wall.

"This way. I'll show you to your room."

The marble steps were wide enough for Maddie to walk next to Giorgio, while he carried her suitcase up the stairs. The second-floor hall was white marble with grey veins running through the large tiles. A Persian rug in shades of greens and blues with cream and gold accents ran down the center of the hallway.

"Your room is the third door on the right," Giorgio said as he opened a white, wooden door trimmed in gold. Maddie walked into a luxurious room. Two windows, almost floor to ceiling, were framed by green-velvet drapes. A king-size, four-poster bed covered with a satin and velvet bedspread in various shades of green stood in the center. Off to one side was an arched entry that led to a sitting room. An antique wood writing desk painted in green with scrolls of gold around pink and yellow flowers faced a French door with a balcony overlooking the garden and the fountain by the front drive. On a table next to the desk was a computer and a printer.

He put her suitcase on a low velvet-upholstered bench at

the foot of the bed. "The armoire in the corner is the wardrobe. The water closet is through that door, or as you say in the States, the bath. There are towels and even a hairdryer—should you care to have a shower. Maybe you would like to take a nap. *Pranzo*, as we say in Italy, or lunch is at two o'clock. I eat with my workers, and I would like you to join us. I must go back to the vineyard, but I'll be home for *pranzo*. The Wi-fi password is *G man*."

"Thank you, Mr. Lombardo."

He looked at her, one dark brow raised. "Giorgio," he said.

"Yes, of course… Giorgio. I would like to get this over with as quickly as possible."

His aqua gaze sparked and held hers. "What? Lunch?"

He was laughing at her. No, he teased and challenged her. Maddie knew it, but the flight had taken its toll. She compressed her lips, holding back a snarky remark.

"We will have time to go over the contract and talk later," Giorgio said, then left the room, closing the door behind him.

Maddie listened to Giorgio whistling an unfamiliar tune as he walked down the hall. His delicious fragrance lingered in the air. She caught herself breathing in the sexy, spicy scent before she opened her case and hung her Valentino pencil skirt in the cedar-lined wardrobe. Then she laid the wide, black-leather belt on a shelf and took another hanger out for the black-silk blouse. Maddie placed her other pair of black stiletto pumps on the wardrobe floor along with her workout shoes. She hung the remainder of her two outfits, the green-silk blouse with the pearl buttons and the other pencil skirt.

She sniffed the air as a whiff of his fragrance lingered before sighing and placing her lingerie in the cedar-lined drawer of the wardrobe, along with her yoga pants and top. Maddie stood her suitcase in the corner of the armoire near her shoes and laid her comfy cotton nightshirt at the foot of the bed. She took the thick file with the contracts and placed them on the desk beside the computer.

A shower would help her relax; she needed to rest so she could be sharp when they negotiated. There was something about Giorgio; he wasn't what she had expected when he'd teased her earlier. Glancing out the window, she saw his matte-black Lamborghini. Now, parked next to it was an old red pickup truck. She watched as Giorgio walked confidently toward the red truck.

He'd changed from the custom-made suit he wore when he picked her up at the airport. Now, he wore denim jeans that even from this distance, accented his narrow hips and muscular legs. *He's got a cute butt.* A blue work shirt stretched across his broad shoulders, the short sleeves hugging his massive biceps. Brown suede lace-up boots completed his work clothes. She watched as he slipped his phone from his pocket and touched the screen. The black roof of the Lamborghini rose from its hiding place.

Maybe he's not arrogant as I first thought when he demanded that a senior bank executive come to him.

In business dealings, Maddie knew she could read people; it was the people in her personal life that she had a difficult time reading.

At the airport, she saw strong confidence in Giorgio and not arrogance. He had left his car at the curb. Then as he loaded her suitcase into the car, a police officer walked over. Maddie thought he was going to give Giorgio a ticket or at the very least, a reprimand. Instead, the officer shook Giorgio's hand and said something in Italian. He stopped the traffic so Giorgio could pull the Lamborghini into the exit lane. There was an inner calmness, but a steel strength as well. A man who knew that when he spoke, people listened and did his bidding without question. He didn't have to show his power; his confidence poured out of his lean, tall, muscled body.

He made Maddie think that maybe not all men were like her ex-fiancé Doug. The man who jilted her, not caring about her feelings. He had used her, and since then, she had become numb to men. Now, she used them.

When she looked at Giorgio, she remembered that *lust* was alive and good for the body. *Sex keeps your skin clear... Business first. What is it they call me behind my back at work? Barracuda. Yes. Business first, Barracuda.*

After her shower, she relaxed on the chaise lounge in her room, listening to music and waiting for lunch or *pranzo,* as Giorgio called it. She looked at the time and decided to head to the patio, where Giorgio had told her to meet him. She walked through the living room to the French doors and out onto the stone patio where an al fresco dining area awaited under an awning of pink blooming bougainvillea. There was a subtle fragrance of rosemary in the air.

Maria and the workers, most of whom wore straw hats and customized t-shirts with the company name, *Lombardo Wines,* over the breast pocket, were already seated and waiting for her and Giorgio. He brought her to the head of the table and pulled out a chair for Maddie. "Please sit. Maria has been cooking all morning." Then he sat next to her.

"It smells wonderful," she said.

Pranzo turned out to be a huge meal. The table was set with colorful linens, ceramic plates, wine glasses, and flatware. Clear glass pitchers of water with fresh slices of lemon floating in them were placed along the center of the table. Next to those were bottles of red and white wine. There was enough food to feed a small village.

They all ate in the open air on the side of the villa. The patio was large and continued around to the back of the house. Maddie saw an infinity pool and spa from the covered patio. Some of the workers spoke English and conversed with Maddie; she wasn't rude but felt utterly out of place in her business attire. Giorgio's work clothes were clean, but the lace-up boots had a dusting of earth on them.

Maybe it would have been wiser to stay at the hotel, Maddie thought.

The first course was served—pasta. The second course was fish with a side of grilled vegetables along with salad, followed by fruit. The wine was wonderful. Giorgio was laughing and talking in Italian to some of the men seated near him. Before he took another bite of his food, he turned to her and asked, "Did you bring any shoes with a lower heel?"

Maddie leaned close to him and whispered, "I didn't know I would be going on a picnic." Then she straightened and said, "I came here to discuss your purchase of the Napa Valley vineyard."

He gave her a smile that melted her before he said, "No business at mealtime. After this, we have *riposo*, rest—"

"Rest?"

"Yes, about two hours where we nap, relax, go for a walk… do *other* things for pleasure."

Maddie didn't miss the innuendo but chose to ignore it. "Between *pranzo* and *riposo*, when do you get any work done?"

"We have plenty of time for work. What do you think all these people have been doing today?" He twirled his pasta onto his fork and took a bite.

Maddie had nothing else to say. She wanted to slap Giorgio's handsome face and wipe that smirk from his lips. Now, all Maddie could think of was the *other* things Giorgio did for pleasure.

Giorgio drank his wine before he said, "Tonight, around

five o'clock, you can give me the contracts to go over... You did bring them?"

"Oh, I brought them, all right." She gritted her teeth, but then she had an idea and said, "Why wait? Let's go over them—"

"No, *Bellissima*... beautiful. Slowly, slowly, after *riposo*."

"Don't call me that," she snapped at him.

His brows furrowed as he said, "Beautiful? I didn't mean it in a derogatory way."

"No. I didn't think that. I... well... let's just say, I *don't* like that term."

"Okay, *Maddalena*. Madeline in Italian, is that good?"

It sounded like a caress. Heat rose in her, and she smiled, looking into his handsome face. "Yes, that's acceptable."

Maria carried out a metal tray with an espresso pot and a platter piled high with pastries for dessert. All Maddie could do was think, *more food*. When they were finished eating, the workers thanked Giorgio and wandered off. She listened as he laughed with some of the men, hearing Giorgio's deep voice above the others. Maria stood and cleared the table. Maddie rose, picking up some of the dishes. "Here, Maria, let me help you."

The modern kitchen blended into the old-world charm of the villa. Even though the older woman repeatedly said, "No. *Grazie.* No," Maddie placed the dirty dishes into a deep farm-style porcelain sink. Maria pointed to a large rectangular, granite-topped table surrounded by six chairs. "Peeze, sit."

"Oh, you do speak English!" Maddie was greeted with Maria's questioning stare.

Maria rinsed the dishes and loaded them into one of the two dishwashers. Maddie found a dishtowel to help dry the larger serving platters and pitchers. As she wiped the ceramic platers, she stacked them on the table. She didn't want to peek into the kitchen cabinets to find where they belonged.

Giorgio walked into the kitchen. His dark hair was damp, and he wore a dark-grey suit with a white shirt and a blue-silk tie that matched the aqua of his eyes. "What are you doing?" He sounded surprised.

"Can't you see? I'm helping Maria. I thought it was obvious," she snarked at him.

He snorted, "Good, then I will leave you. I'm going to my office in Palermo. A matter arose… I should be back around eight."

She slammed the dishtowel down on the table and looked at him. "Eight o'clock in the evening?" Her astonishment couldn't be hidden.

"Yes, tonight around eight."

"But… wait. I thought you were going to do that *riposo* thing you spoke about? I'll get the contracts; we can sign them before you leave."

"I have *other* things I have to take care of. Why don't you go rest, and then when I get back, we can look at them and go from there?"

He was proving to be very annoying. But Maddie was tired and went up to her room. She popped in her ear pods and lay on the chaise lounge to listen to some music. She must have dozed, because when she awoke, the time display on her phone read six thirty. Maddie showered and dried her hair and then coiled it into a messy bun. She applied a thin line of eyeliner and a swipe of mascara to her lashes. Then she slicked on some lipstick and pinched her cheeks for color. Maddie changed into her black pencil skirt and matching silk blouse with the sheer sleeves to wear for dinner.

At precisely eight o'clock, she heard the engine of his Lamborghini and went down the marble steps. By the time she reached the living room, he walked into the entry. Giorgio's handsome face, with a day's growth of beard, made her breath hitch. *Pirate*, she thought.

"Hi, I see you're ready. Did you have a good rest?"

"Yes, thanks. Now I'm ready to negotiate the sale of the vineyard."

"We will, but first, I asked Maria to set up dinner for us. We can eat in the barrel room."

Surprised by that, she said, "The building you pointed out earlier? The one in the fields?" Maddie ran her hands down her skintight skirt. She watched as his eyes followed and continued all the way to her black-leather stiletto pumps. Her heart thudded as his gaze slowly rose to meet her eyes.

"No worries," he said. "We will drive over in my car."

CHAPTER 2

Giorgio pulled up to the stone structure that he called the barrel room. The exterior was lit with old-style, coach lanterns. The double wooden doors were stained in a light-maple color with heavy black-iron hinges and two antique-looking knobs. Above the entry hung a weathered plaque; the faded words were written in Italian.

"What does that say?" Maddie asked.

"Good food. Good wine. Good friends," Giorgio said as he pushed open one side of the double doors and switched on the interior lights.

The floor was made of stone in deep earth colors leading down a large corridor. As Maddie walked into the coolness of the building, the aroma of grapes and wine delighted her senses. The stone and brick building he'd called the barrel room was actually more than one room, she realized as they walked down a corridor to another room. Through the large arched entry laid rows and rows of barrels, stacked three high. "These barrels are filled with wine that are in different stages of the aging process," he said as he led her to a table set with an arrangement of flowers and candles. The first sign of a romantic dinner.

It had to be the aroma of the wine, she thought as she walked over and ran her finger on the white damask cloth covering the intimate round table. The faint fragrance of roses and candle flame filled her nostrils as she stared up into his aqua eyes that gave nothing away. She wouldn't back down from a challenge.

"Wow, the women you bring here must love this." She looked around and smirked, "Do you have a bed hidden somewhere among the barrels?"

He raised a brow and gave her a look that she read as 'I know you aren't as tough as you want me to believe.'

Giorgio smiled and said, "You're the first."

That annoyed her. "You think men are the end all? That we women can't live without a man? Well, let me tell you, *Mr. Lombardo,* I don't need a man for any reason." She ignored the tightening of her nipples. The pulsing between her legs reminded her that it was a lie. Giorgio made her think of all the wonderful things she hadn't done in quite a while.

"Maybe what you need is right before your eyes," Giorgio said. The challenge was in his words. Written on his gorgeous, arrogant face, and in the depths of his aqua eyes, just waiting for her to accept.

A little breathless laugh escaped Maddie as she realized he wouldn't be one to run from a challenge. She straightened her spine and said, "Oh? What's the word I'm looking for?"

"Lust," he interjected.

His deep voice vibrated into her core. "It all boils down to sex for your type. Well, I don't think so!" she said.

He raised one of his thick, perfectly shaped brows, and, in a husky voice, he said, "I haven't asked."

That infuriated her. "*I don't* need a man for any reason." Oh, the audacity of him to make it sound as if she were the one wanting him inside her body... touching her... running his tongue along her body, licking her.

"It isn't all about work, *Maddalena*. We know how to live and enjoy life. You know that quaint American saying—stop and smell the roses? Well, here in Sicily, we do that on a regular basis. Enjoy life, live, and yes... love."

He exasperated her, making her think how nice to see her fingernail marks on that handsome face. No! Down his back. Yes... well... maybe that... or better yet, her feet on his broad shoulders as he put his tongue into her, making her climax.

Maddie gasped when she realized what she was thinking and tried desperately to stop the thoughts running through her head. It had been too long since she'd let a man touch her and five years since Doug left her. Here she was. And all Giorgio had to do was look at her, and her blood sizzled through her veins. Maddie knew she'd strip for him and lay on the floor right here in the barrel room. All Giorgio would have to do is snap his fingers.

"Well, *are* we going to have dinner?" she snarked, trying to cover the excitement she felt.

He smiled a lazy grin at her. "Of course, please sit."

Giorgio watched as Maddie squared her shoulders, her chin jutted out, taking on a no-nonsense attitude as she walked to her seat in those towering stiletto heels. *Her cute butt swings so sexily. She probably doesn't realize what a hard-on she's giving me. This Madeline Watson certainly has spunk. I like that. Business is the last thing I want to talk about with her. What I want requires no talking at all.*

Giorgio could deal with tough women; after all, with a mother like his, he needed to. The chair scraped on the stone floor as he pulled it out for Maddie. He poured the deep-red-colored wine into both glasses and served a very traditional dish of baked macaroni.

He knew Maddie didn't understand the significance of that particular meal. It was served on Sundays or when special guests were over. Maria's eyes had rounded when he had requested she prepare the dish. Now, he sat opposite Maddie in the dim, flickering light from the candles. He admired her beauty.

"Tell me why you came here," Giorgio asked. "You said that you usually work in Tokyo. Why did the bank send you?"

Maddie put her fork down. "Once you made it clear that you required a senior bank executive, someone who could make decisions, I think those were your exact words... At this time, my father... is unable to travel, and my brother is the acting bank president. I had worked in loss mitigation before I moved to Japan, so... they asked me to do this."

"Thank you. It was impossible for me to get away at this time," he said.

Giorgio and Maddie both seemed to dance around the issue, neither willing to give an inch. "How long have you been working this vineyard?"

He liked the way she snarked at him. She was smooth, he thought, but then the amusement fled as he said, "Since I was young, after my father died. My mother was still in her teens when she'd married my father... but after he suddenly died... she hated this place. She couldn't wait to get away from here. My paternal grandmother," a smile softened his expression, "took over the vineyard, waiting until I could inherit it. My mother bought a townhouse in Palermo, where we both lived."

He smirked as he remembered his mother's frustration. "DiMarco Enterprises was jointly run by my father and my Uncle Giuseppe DiMarco, my mother's brother. But she wasn't satisfied after my father passed; she demanded her rightful place in the company. The only problem was that women weren't able to head companies… or hold office. Their place… was in the home, making babies."

He laughed at Maddie's horrified expression. He hadn't meant to, but her beautiful face contorted with a mix of anger and disbelief.

"Now, *Maddalena*, I hope you realize that I don't have the same thoughts."

Her perfectly shaped brows furrowed, and she nodded. "I know you aren't the CEO; is that what your mother wanted for you?"

He shrugged a shoulder. "I wouldn't know what she wanted. My uncle provided for her; after all, she is a DiMarco. He kept my inheritance secure for me and treated me just the same as his sons, guiding me in my schooling and university choices. My cousin Ricardo is the CEO and a damn good one."

He watched Maddie as her frown disappeared, and she sipped her wine. When she took another bite of her food, Giorgio outstretched his arms. Leaning back, the front legs of his chair lifted from the stone floor. "I enjoy this, making wine, buying vineyards." He dropped his arms and the chair at the same time, then picked up his fork. "In Italy, France, Spain, and even South America, expanding the business. I get to travel and see the world. I go to board meetings as one of the executives of DiMarco Enterprises and president of Lombardo Wines… Soon, I will include California—"

She lifted her gaze to his. "We haven't signed the agreement yet. When we finish eating this delicious meal, let's go back to the villa and get the papers—"

Giorgio held her moss-green gaze. "What do you like?" he said as he glanced at her lips.

"I enjoy working in finance," she said firmly.

He smiled at the way she chose to ignore his implication. He put his linen napkin on the table beside his dish. "Would you care for… more?"

"No, thanks. I would like to get the contracts and proceed with the deal."

He stood. "Certainly, but let's have a brandy back at the villa."

She walked next to him and even in those towering heels of hers, he was at least six inches taller than she. They drove the short distance in silence, then Giorgio came around his car to open her door and led her into the dimly lit entry. "Watch your step!"

His hand shot out to grab her arm as she tripped, but he missed. He smirked. *Women drop at my feet all the time. She is no different, on her knees before me.*

Maddie gazed up, her moss-green eyes wide, and her peach-tinted lips parted as her small, pink tongue moistened her full bottom lip. Giorgio felt a stirring as lust shot through his blood, into his groin, fully arousing him. He reached a hand toward his zipper. *No!* his brain screamed as he reached out to lift her to her feet.

He growled between gritted teeth, "Didn't you bring any other shoes?" *Oh… to feel her lips, her tongue on me… take me into her mouth…*

Maddie brushed her pencil skirt with one hand as she snarked, "Wow, I haven't fallen in ages. And there I was, kneeling at your feet." She shook her head, her cheeks red.

Giorgio knew *Maddie* would be the one to have *him* on *his* knees, worshiping her.

He laughed a deep belly laugh. "Too bad, I didn't wish to take advantage." He led the way into the living room. Indicating the brown-leather sofa, he said, "Have a seat. Is brandy good?"

"Yes," she replied as she sat.

He shrugged out of his jacket and loosened his tie, opening two of his collar buttons. Giorgio poured two glasses of liquor and brought her one. He sat in the wing chair opposite the sofa where Maddie sat. The weather was far too warm for a fire, but this time of the year, his house-keeper liked to keep fresh flowers, from the garden in the hearth, perfuming the room.

～

MADDIE TRIED NOT to stare at him. Giorgio sat, resting one elbow on the arm of his leather chair. He held the crystal brandy glass loosely, the stem between two lean fingers in the palm of his hand. Giorgio raised the glass and ran his thumb slowly back and forth along the side before he tipped it to his sculpted lips. His five o'clock shadow gave him a definite bad boy look.

Maddie took a sip of the brandy, picking up the conversation from before she had clumsily tripped. "I moved back to LA a month ago. I'd gone to live in Tokyo five years ago… after—"

She couldn't believe what she was about to say. Maddie gazed up into aqua eyes and saw compassion in the depths, compelling her to talk. "I was jilted and wanted to get out of LA. So, I went to live in Tokyo."

He looked surprised and then asked, "Why Japan?"

"I'd studied Japanese in college and with my banking background, I obtained a position at an international bank in their finance department…" She glanced into the distance as she said, "Now that I think about it… I know that I really had run away," she shrugged. "He married… my best friend."

Why did she feel so comfortable with this stranger? It was his eyes. Those deep-aqua eyes, so full of compassion. They said they were listening to her, not just seeing her.

Maddie composed herself and looked at Giorgio. "The night before the big church wedding, he'd come to tell me that he didn't want to marry me. He was in love with someone else. He loved Nancy, my best friend from childhood, *and* my maid of honor."

Maddie shook her head. To this day, it continued to irk her—how her best friend had deceived her. "They had been scheming to go away... and... then... they went on the honeymoon I had planned for Doug and me."

She compressed her lips and with an ever so slight shrug, she tipped her head to the side and said, "I was the one left to tell everyone. It was too late to cancel the reception, and well, I felt obligated to go and tell our pastor. The following morning, I drove to the church—where I would have been married and explained what had happened. Doug hadn't bothered to say anything, he left it all to me." She took a sip of her drink, before continuing, "My brother and father handled the guests who came to the church. My mother arranged to return all the wedding gifts. I managed to get through it all, and then I left... He still works at the bank in the legal department." She raised a shoulder. "Once I left, I guess he felt it was okay to stay on."

Giorgio saw the unspoken pain that glinted in her moss-green eyes. What she said made everything fall into place. The tough girl act, the bank executive with a heart of stone. It wasn't stone. Maddie was protecting herself; that's what it was. To have the person she loved discard her in such a manner. A strange feeling barely registered in the deepest recesses of his mind, he wanted to protect her. Giorgio never wanted her to feel the pain of rejection and abandonment again. He most definitely wanted to kiss away her hurt—

until her only thought would be of him. An urge to bury himself in her and soothe all her wounds gripped him.

He squashed those feelings as quickly as they surfaced and poured more brandy into her glass, then sat next to her. She told him of her work, but particularly of how she loved to ride horses. Taking lessons since she was seven years old and how she competed in shows.

The grandfather clock in the entry chimed four a.m. "Oh my, it's really late. You've made me ramble on about nothing of importance," she said.

He leaned close to her. Maddie's jasmine scent floated around him and in a low voice, he said, "It's not nonsense. Being away from your family, that had to be a challenging and painful time in your life."

"I survived." She shrugged.

"It's late, and you need to rest. In the morning, we can look at the contracts," Giorgio said in a soft voice.

Maddie didn't argue with him. Instead, she said, "I must apologize for going on and on about my private life."

"Don't. I won't think less of you. You are a complete professional, and I enjoyed hearing about you competing with your horse."

Her scent filled his nostrils, and he fought the urge to pull the pins from her bun and feel the silky tresses. They walked up the steps, and at her bedroom door, Giorgio stopped. "Go get the contracts. I'll take them to my study. If I have any questions, we can discuss them in the morning."

Maddie went into her room and quickly came back with the file. "I did my due diligence, Mr. Lombardo. You'll notice that I have included a counteroffer, increasing your original offer price by ten percent." She handed the folder to Giorgio. "If you want, we can go over them now, then I would be able to make arrangements to fly back to LA."

Maddie saw a glint in his aqua eyes. The slight nod of his

head and admiration in his glance before finally lifting the corners of that oh-so-gorgeous mouth into a smile. "No, tomorrow is soon enough. *Buona notte, Maddalena.*" He took the contracts from her hand and walked out of the room, closing the door behind him.

At least he knows I'm not a pushover. The increase is still a good deal on that property.

The doorknob clicking into place sounded so loud in the silence of her room. Maddie reached and turned the lock. A heaviness settled between her legs. She still had sex. After all, wasn't that a biological necessity? Well… if she were honest with herself, biology was at a standstill. She hadn't been with anyone for some time, actually not since Maui, and that was last December.

She tried touching herself and found that lacking, impersonal, so she immersed herself in work, the same as she had done all those years living in Japan with just the occasional hookup. Now, Giorgio made her core pulse and throb. She shook her head, then slipped on her old, comfortable, cotton nightshirt and crawled into bed.

In the morning, when Maddie woke, she showered and dressed. Then she went in search of Giorgio. She knew he was a shrewd businessman, and his cash offer was enticing. She may have to argue for the additional ten percent. *What would that be, the cost of his Lamborghini?*

Maddie found Maria in the kitchen. "Good morning, do you know where Mr. Lombardo is?"

"Buon giorno, café?"

"Coffee. Yes. Thank you. Mr. Lombardo?"

The older woman reached into the pocket of her blue apron and handed Maddie a folded piece of paper. Maddie unfolded it and read the scribble.

I had to go to Palermo. I expect to be back for pranzo.

G.

She crumpled the paper, turned to Maria in frustration, and asked for the phone. The older woman didn't understand. So, Maddie tried pantomime. Holding her thumb close to her ear and her pinky near her lips, she said, "Telephone—Giorgio… c-a-l-l- Giorgio."

Maria's eyes lit with comprehension. "*Si, si. Telefono* Giorgio." She hurried to the hall phone and dialed a number. Maria spoke into the phone and then handed it to Maddie.

"Hello," she said into the phone.

"Hey, you finally woke up." Giorgio's husky voice breathed into her ear.

"I thought we were going to negotiate this deal," she said in a rush. "I *have* to get back to LA. I can't play around here—"

"It's done," Giorgio said. "My bank has the order to wire the money as we speak. Once you and I sign the contracts, Maria can be a witness to that. Then I will have my bank release the funds. I feel your price increase was fair. I looked over the appraisal you brought and the one I had *my* attorney perform, along with the most recent soil report I had ordered before I made the offer. I feel this is a good deal for both Lombardo Wines and Watson Financial. I'll be back for pranzo."

Maddie looked at the phone. *Why the hell did I fly here? I didn't need to travel halfway around the world to—Oh, he is the most insufferable man.* Into the phone, she said, "Okay. I… I'll be here. Although, Giorgio, I don't know why I came all this way." She ended the call, took her coffee, thanked Maria, and went upstairs to her room.

Anger and frustration collided inside her. He was the most annoying man she'd ever met. She had to calm down. She sat on the floor and did some yoga in her room. Then she worked on two of her clients' portfolios. One client needed cash and wanted to liquidate. She divided his portfolio into long-term and short-term assets so she could analyze and advise him on the best approach to avoid losing too much money. Her other client came to her recently from another financial advisor. He wanted more diversity but less risk. Those two files kept her busy through the morning and up until lunchtime.

Giorgio did come back home in time for *pranzo* looking smug in one of his custom-made suits. He shrugged out of the jacket, his sexy cologne subtly floating through the air, reaching her nostrils. He loosened his blue-silk tie, opening the top button of his white shirt, and said, "Are you hungry?"

For you to unbutton the rest of your shirt. "Maria's cooking smells delicious," Maddie said.

"I'm sure Maria has set everything up on the patio," Giorgio said.

They walked out from the living room's double French doors onto the stone patio. Just as yesterday, the workers were seated around the long table waiting for Giorgio. Almost in unison, they said hello to her.

Maddie smiled. "Hello all."

The awning of bougainvillea shaded the patio in the mild Sicilian afternoon. Maddie sat at the table next to Giorgio, leaning toward him as she asked, "Do you have any ice for the water?"

He gazed at her, a smile crinkling the corners of his eyes as he said, "We don't use ice."

Surprised by that, all she could say was. "Really?"

Giorgio leaned close to her before he said, "I'll ask Maria to make some. They'll be ready before dinner this evening."

She didn't have much else to say and applied herself to the delicious meal Maria had prepared. Pasta naturally, but what a dish. Giorgio had called it *pasta alla Norma.* It was made with fresh tomatoes, eggplant, and basil, combined to make the most flavorful meal she'd had in a long time. Once the main course was over, Maria brought out a platter of cannoli and a pot of espresso. Giorgio joked with some of his men, and then they wandered off. The men tipped their hats to her, and she wished them a good afternoon.

After lunch, she and Giorgio signed the contract.

"I would like to overnight the original contract and the deed to our attorney in California, so the title company can record the purchase in Napa Valley," Maddie said. "Will you be able to have a courier here today?"

He flashed Maddie one of those smiles that had her pulse racing before he said, "I have taken care of that. The messenger is here waiting in my study."

"Good. Let's get this over with." *Before I jump on you.* She turned on her stilettos and followed Giorgio.

Once the package was on its way, Giorgio turned to Maddie. "It's a beautiful afternoon, not too hot. You said you're an equestrian. I have a stable here on the property. Would you like to go for a ride?"

"I thought you had to go back to the vineyard."

"The critical time for the grapes has passed, and my workers can do the rest for today, without me breathing down their necks."

You can breathe on my neck. What is my problem today? "I would enjoy a ride very much. Do you have sunblock?"

She watched his gaze travel over her face before he said, "Yes, you're very fair. I'll ask Maria to bring some to your room… Later, we can drive into Palermo so you can see some of the city before you return home."

I WOULD LOVE to see your naked body, feel your cock in me, she thought. *Why do I turn everything he says into a sexual innuendo?* "I would like that. I'll go change."

She went upstairs and put on her pink yoga pants and

matching tankini, laced her sport sneakers, and applied the sunblock. She grabbed her designer sunglasses and sunhat, then went downstairs. Giorgio had said for her to meet him in the living room when she was ready. He stood near a window, looking outside.

"Hello," she said.

He turned from the window. *Oh God,* she groaned, looking at him, her gaze traveling to his fawn-colored riding pants. They were molded to his lower body, showing every bulge and defining every muscle. His narrow hips, the power of his thighs, his—*no, don't look there*—Finally, her eyes moved down to his black knee-high riding boots. She was going to embarrass herself as she stared at his lower body.

"Ready?" he asked.

Only then did she glance up to see his smile. "We can take the truck," he said, his aqua eyes burning into her.

Her cheeks felt flushed. Her throat was dry. She barely nodded as they walked out the front door of his home to the circular drive. Maddie fought the urge to fan her cheeks and climbed into the red pickup truck. He turned the key in the ignition, and the motor started.

"It's not too far to the stables. I called ahead, so the horses should be ready."

"Stables?" she asked, surprised. "How many horses do you have?"

"The barn is on my property, but some of the horses belong to my uncle and my cousins. We keep fifteen horses there. Six of them are mine."

"Wow! That's great. I own one, and I just recently brought him over from Hawaii and board him at the stable where I rode as a kid."

"You lived in Tokyo and boarded your horse in Hawaii?"

"I know it sounds funny, but it was sort of a halfway

point. I would meet my family on Maui... so... I didn't have to go back to LA."

"That makes sense," Giorgio said.

He stopped the truck by the barn where a groom held the reins of two horses. They were both saddled and ready for them. A black stallion and a bay-colored horse. Maddie touched the muzzle of the bay-colored stallion.

"You're such a handsome boy," she said. Then glancing at Giorgio, she giggled. "Does he understand English?"

"He most definitely understands the gentle touch of your hand." Maddie hid her response to his words, ignoring the zing of pleasure that went through her body. They rode through the rolling hills of the vineyard and down to a watering hole. "This land belonged to my father's family. My father planted many of these vines, expanding the vineyard," Giorgio said, his voice had an air of pride in it.

The warmth of the sun touched Maddie as she gazed at the beautiful scenery. The vineyard was busy with workers, some filling baskets with purple grape clusters, while others carted the straw baskets of grapes to place on flatbed trucks. Surrounded by all the activities, Maddie saw the ruin of an ancient home among some cottages scattered over his property. "What happened over there? That home lost its roof."

"My great-great-grandparents lived in that home. It was temporary while they built the villa I live in now. My father was born in the villa, and so was I."

She and Giorgio had a pleasant afternoon riding through the rolling hills of the vineyard. He joked about her choice of riding outfit.

"I'm thrilled that I brought my yoga pants. I didn't think I would have needed my jodhpurs." She blushed.

"Let's go back to the villa. You can rest and get ready, so we can go into Palermo."

The house was quiet when they walked in. Maddie went

up to her room to shower and change into her black pencil skirt and silk blouse. She put on her stilettos and grabbed her jacket. She met Giorgio in the entry. He'd changed into a navy-blue suit, his white shirt, and baby-blue-colored tie. The clip holding his tie and cufflinks were engraved with his initials.

Giorgio drove through the city, taking Maddie to some of the typical tourist spots, pointing out some interesting facts. Then he asked her if she would like to eat dinner out. When she said yes, he called Maria and told her not to cook for them or bother waiting up.

"Do you always eat this late in the evening?" Maddie asked. "It's after nine o'clock."

"Yes, we do here in Italy, but we don't have a very heavy meal."

The evening weather was mild, and Giorgio had asked if she would like to eat at a restaurant on the beach. "I love the beach. I actually live on the beach in Malibu." They walked into a restaurant, and the hostess welcomed him by name. Giorgio spoke to the hostess, and then she seated them out on the veranda.

A waiter came over, and Giorgio asked Maddie, "Do you trust me to order? The food here is delicious. It's street food and great wine. Or beer if you prefer."

"I'm pretty easy," Maddie said. *Oh God, that sounded terrible.* "Wine is good," she quickly added.

Giorgio raised a brow, and a smile played around his lips. He turned to the waiter and ordered their meal. When the waiter left, Giorgio said, "I know a club where they play American music. We could go after dinner if you would like to go dancing."

Was this a date? She had two rules that she never broke. *One. No sleeping the whole night with a man. Two. No dating. Ever! No complications, just sex.*

"I… would… like that very much," she found herself saying.

Giorgio drove to an area he called *Mondello*. It was another beach town, and the club was different from the ones in LA, and definitely not like the ones in Tokyo.

It was so nice to be able to dance out in the open and not worry about super-huge crowds. The club was loud and the atmosphere fun and electrifying. She had a great time with Giorgio. He knew all the latest dance moves, and they danced to some great American songs. At one point, Giorgio said, "This place winds down around three in the morning. It's already two; do you want to go?"

"Yes, I'm beat."

When they arrived back at his house, he walked her upstairs to her bedroom. At the door, she said, "Good night and thank you. I had a great time."

Giorgio bent and kissed her on the forehead. "*Buona notte,* Madeline."

CHAPTER 3

The early-morning sun streamed through the living room window, turning Giorgio's hair mahogany. Maddie was dressed and ready to go to his lawyer's office, though they had come to terms on the deal yesterday. Giorgio had dispatched the wire transfer to Watson Financial late in the day, before they'd gone out to dinner and dancing. Now, they were waiting for confirmation on that. They had signed the agreement with Maria as a witness. The hard copies of the documents were overnighted to California. Going to Giorgio's attorney had become a formality and wasn't necessary. Maddie had power of attorney for this deal, and Giorgio was the president of Lombardo Wines, a part of DiMarco Enterprises.

She decided that perhaps there was something else they could do while waiting for the confirmation of the wire transfer. Once they were notified, she could make arrangements to catch a flight to Rome and then on to LA.

She smiled demurely at Giorgio, thinking, *what must he look like naked. All those muscles... his broad shoulders.* She didn't think he was very hairy, which was good; she didn't like men with a lot of hair. She had learned a long time ago that she didn't need to be in love to have sex. She only needed the other L-word. Lust. If only he knew what she was thinking.

"Well, why don't we—" Giorgio started.

Maddie toyed with the top button of her green-silk blouse and took a step. Giorgio stopped mid-sentence. His black brows came together, and he leaned his hip against the windowsill as Maddie moved forward, her fingers working the tiny pearl button.

She moved toward him as her fingers reached for the next button. The space between them seemed to evaporate in the heat from her body. Giorgio casually unbuttoned his suit jacket. She glanced at his narrow waist and further down. Giorgio's legs reminded Maddie of tree trunks covered by the expensive material of his custom-made suit. The muscles of his thighs bunched under the charcoal-grey fabric.

She slipped a third pearl button through the hole. He pursed his lips and raised one dark eyebrow. Another button and another opened, revealing the lacy bra that barely covered the crests of her breasts. A slow smile spread across his sensuous lips.

Giorgio didn't move as Maddie sauntered over, stopping a few inches from him, not touching him. She leaned in, the sexy spice of his scent filling her head.

She whispered, "How much time do you think we have before they realize we're not going to make the meeting?"

His lips spread, showing Maddie his even, white teeth and his brilliant smile. Smoldering aqua eyes dropped to look at her breasts then back to hold her gaze. The heat between them was scorching as he said, with his oh-so-slight Italian accent, "We have as much time as you want."

Maddie didn't answer as her core pulsed. She pulled the

green-silk blouse out of her cream-colored waistband, slipping her arms out of the short sleeves. The silk garment silently fell to the marble floor. She ran the tip of her tongue along her top lip, and her fingers moved to the center of her sheer-lace bra. Between the valley of her breasts, she unhooked the material and brushed the thin straps down her arms and let the lacy bra join her blouse on his living room floor.

Giorgio's eyes burned into her; she knew he wouldn't make this easy. It thrilled her. She felt excitement spreading between her legs, getting ready for him. Her breasts ached to feel his hands, his sculpted lips. Would he nibble on her flesh? Her nipples tightened.

Instinct told her he would be huge, and she needed that so very much. Maddie reached her hands behind her, making her breasts rise, offering them to his gaze as she unzipped the skin-tight skirt, shimmying the material down past her hips and let it fall to her feet. Standing before him in her panties and silk stockings, his gaze burned her.

He said, "I guess we're going to be very, very late."

Giorgio bent slightly to scoop her into his powerful arms. "I think we should continue this upstairs in my bedroom." He nuzzled her lips. "What do you think?"

Maddie smiled, and her hands were at his tie, her fingers loosening the knot. He was at the marble steps, and even before Giorgio put his Italian leather-shod foot on the first tread, she pulled the blue-silk tie through his shirt collar, letting it dangle from her fingers for a heartbeat before it silently fell to the floor. Next, she reached for the buttons of his white-silk shirt as she breathed in his wonderful scent, cologne and virile man.

By the time he reached the second-floor landing, she had opened his shirt, her hands rubbing his broad chest, smiling at the mat of dark hair covering the muscles, playing with his flat nipples. One more flight, and they reached his bedroom. He shouldered his door open and walked in. Giorgio laid her in the center of his gigantic four-poster bed. He straightened and looked at her.

"*Dio mio*, you are a seductress. Take your panties and stockings off," he demanded in his husky voice.

Giorgio walked on the blue and cream Persian rug back to the door and turned the latch on the gold-toned handle. He shrugged out of his jacket and shirt, laying them on an accent chair by the fireplace. Kicking his shoes off at the same time. The rasp of his zipper made Maddie's center pulse as his slacks fell to the floor, along with his black-silk boxers. He left those on the floor and turned to come to the bed.

He *was* huge. And those perfectly formed broad shoulders, his arms were sculpted with bulging muscles. His pecks, his abdomen, and narrow hips. His legs, his thighs defined by more muscles, and that most beautiful part of him jutting out. *I'm going to come just looking at him.*

Giorgio was a drug to Maddie—one she never wanted to stop taking and hadn't even realized she needed. Maddie breathed a slow yoga breath, she had to be strong. After all, she was going home. *Just this once, and he'll be out of my mind.* Did she hear herself? The contradiction was apparent to her subconscious. But all she wanted was him between her legs, soothing the ache that had begun the moment she saw him at the airport.

His mouth... his pulsing erection. Maddie was so involved with looking at him that she forgot he asked her to take off her panties and stockings. Lifting her buttocks off the cool, crisp sheets, she slid the thin elastic and sheer panties down her legs and off. Then she lifted one leg in the air and rolled the thigh-high stocking down and off her foot.

She did the same with the other. Maddie had kicked her shoes off somewhere between the second floor and his bedroom.

She lay on his bed naked and so hot. Desire coursing through her veins. His aqua eyes with their gold flecks shooting fire right into her core. Maddie was sure he knew how to please women—and somehow the thought of him with other women disturbed her. The smile on his face as he looked at her made Maddie think how carefree he was, but also how confident. Giorgio came to the bed naked, muscles rippling, and leaned one knee on the mattress, reminding Maddie of the throbbing need she felt.

He smiled down at her and touched her cheek with one of his strong hands. "Why now?"

She rubbed her cheek into his palm. "I need you."

"What do you want, my sweet Maddalena? Tell me."

Maddie, brazen as always, took her pointing finger and ran it along the length of his cock. He was fully aroused, and her fingertip lingered on the velvety smooth head. "I would love for you and me to take the lust we feel and have some fun. Just lusting, Giorgio."

"FUN? *STREGA*, WITCH." He reached around her and lifted her torso off the bed, bringing her breasts in contact with his chest. "You want to have fun? I'm all for fun."

He reached down and slid a finger along the blonde tuft of hair parting her damp curls. Maddie opened her legs, her hands gripping his biceps. Sliding up to his shoulders, she pulled him closer. Her fingers pushed into the hair at the nape of his neck, and she reached her parted lips up to his mouth. His kiss began softly, teasing her lips. Her kiss was hot with desire. Giorgio groaned inwardly and cradled her head as he took control of the kiss that inflamed his soul.

Her small tongue tasted like heaven in his mouth as it entwined with his, then retreated. He followed, possessing her sweet mouth adoring her feel, her taste. Giorgio broke the kiss with a nibble on her lower lip before he kissed and licked the satin-soft skin of her neck, breathing in her intoxicating scent. He took the lobe of her ear into his mouth, touching his tongue to the soft flesh. Maddie moaned.

And all Giorgio wanted was to grab her hips, spread her legs, and thrust into her heat. The seductive sounds she made had been driving him crazy, but he wanted to thoroughly enjoy this woman. Fighting for control took an effort. Still, he wouldn't use her only to satisfy himself; he wanted her as he had never wanted another woman.

When he pressed his lips to hers—heaven. Her mouth was pure honey. Their tongues sparring, he encouraged Maddie to lead, holding her tighter in his arms. Giorgio rolled onto his back, taking her beautiful body with him. She smothered a gasp and giggled in that seductive, throaty way that was only hers.

Maddie spread her fingers on his chest as she raised herself a tiny bit. Sliding her open hands down along to his waist, her hands caressed his muscles. She moved up his body and straddled his abdomen as he reached for her breasts, gently squeezing her hard nipples. Playing with them between his thumbs and forefingers.

She threw back her head and then came forward, moving higher on his torso, offering her breasts to his hungering mouth. Giorgio took what she gave and drew one nipple into his mouth. His tongue learned the texture of her breast, and his lips drew on her feeling the nipple extend into a hard bud. She bucked forward, and he held her other breast in his hand, molding it in his palm and playing with the nipple.

Maddie closed her hand around his erection and gently squeezed. Giorgio let go of the nipple.

"I see you don't want to go slow." He stretched his arm out and reached over to the nightstand, opening a drawer to grab a condom. "So, let's get this on me."

He ripped open the packet as Maddie scooted on his strong body so he could roll the condom on. Holding Maddie's slight curves to him, he slid up the bed, leaning against the massive wooden headboard and reclining on the pillows.

She gave another throaty laugh, and her knees fell to either side of his body. Giorgio held her tiny waist. Gazing into those moss-green eyes, he positioned her over his throbbing erection. She held his gaze as he guided her dripping-wet center over him. He teased her folds and then lowered her down as he stroked up into searing heat.

Her husky laugh turned into a moan as her lids closed over her moss-green eyes, with her lips raised at the corners into a satisfied smile. "Mmm... hmm, how wonderful you feel in me... *So* big."

"Your heat is melting the condom," he said.

Maddie giggled as she straddled him, rotating her hips in slow circles. Giorgio slid his fingers into the silky strands of her hair, cupping her head, and pulled her down to his mouth. Needing to kiss those lips, her mouth opened to his, and he ran his tongue along her teeth. She sucked his tongue into her mouth. Maddie sank all the way down, taking all of his thick length into her heat. She rocked back and forward, arching her spine.

He loved it, meeting each and every one of her demands. His hands moved down the curve of her back, feeling each vertebra along the way. Sliding his hands to her buttocks and around to her flaring hips, he pulled her closer to him. He thrust up and pushed her down on his length, her heat surrounded him. Giorgio held back the shout of pleasure her body brought him.

Maddie's head fell back, her long, blonde hair brushing his thighs. Giorgio sucked a turgid nipple into his mouth. Her fingers tangled in his hair, and she held him to her as he nibbled on the bud. Giorgio traced a path along the satin skin to her other nipple.

Maddie raised and lowered herself on his erection, riding him in a frenzy of need. Her muscles gripped him in the most exquisite torture. She whimpered, and with every breathy moan, she excited him as no other woman ever had.

"Ohhh, ahhh… yes… yesss…" Maddie panted, grinding her hips.

Giorgio held the firm mound of her breast in his hand and sucked on her pointed nipple.

"Yes, make me come," she yelled between puffs of breath.

He traced a path over her abdomen into the soft, blonde curls, and his middle finger found her swollen clit.

"Yes, oh God, yes, Giorgio. That feels sooo good." She moved faster.

He held his finger on her clit, applying slight pressure and small manipulations. "You are so tight and hot… I want to feel you come all around me."

Giorgio gritted his teeth, trying for control. His words were all it took to send Maddie over the edge. The scream that escaped her filled him with more pleasure than he had ever experienced as he pumped up into her, reaching a mind-shattering climax of his own.

Maddie fell forward on Giorgio's chest, her spasms like little aftershocks going on and on. When they subsided, he brushed her mass of golden hair from her face. He reached for her rounded hips and smiling, he gazed into her passion-filled eyes.

"Feel me? I'm ready for more." Giorgio lifted her and then slid Maddie down his hard length.

She moaned as a new set of contractions squeezed him. He touched her clit, rubbing her slick flesh back and forth, touching, exploring, and finding where she was most sensitive. He made her climax again, and she laughed in her pleasure. Giorgio felt each ripple of her laughter around him. He had never experienced anyone as wild as Madeline Watson. She moved to his side, running her fingers through his chest hair. Giorgio kissed her lips, lingering on a corner.

"I will be right back," he whispered before he got off the bed. He padded to the bathroom and disposed of the condom.

When he came back to her, she'd pushed the bedspread to the foot of the bed. Giorgio took another condom from the drawer and lay next to Maddie, kissing those luscious lips of hers, getting lost in her sensuous body. He kissed her neck, holding her breast in one hand, playing with the nipple. He rolled with her, so she lay on her back. Kissing her throat, feeling her pulse under his lips, he rained kisses down to her collarbone, lingering there before sliding his tongue along the satin skin to suck a pointed nipple into his mouth. She reached for him as he lay in the cradle of her open thighs. Giorgio stopped long enough to grab for the condom.

Maddie played with his flat nipples, running her fingers through his chest hair. She traced the thin line of black hair down to his abdomen. She lay under him, her blonde hair a mass of tangles spread out on his pillow. Her jasmine scent reached his nostrils. Her breasts pink from his kisses, the nipples swollen. She spread her smooth, creamy, white thighs wider as she reached for his buttocks, pressing him.

Giorgio slipped his arms under her knees, catching them at his elbows. Holding Maddie open, he thrust deep into her tight passage, moving side to side. Maddie's lids slipped down, her sooty lashes laid on her cheeks, and her lips parted. Her head fell into the pillows as her neck arched. Maddie's long, blonde hair in a tangle of wild curls spread across his pillow.

Giorgio stroked his way in and out of her wet heat. He pistoned faster and faster as she held him, her nails digging into his buttocks. Her head rolled on the pillow. She made a mewling sound that he learned she made just before she climaxed.

"Ahh. Yes. I'm mmm… Ohhh."

Her orgasm stroked him. "*Strega.* You are a witch," he said, staying deep in her as the walls of her vagina continued to caress him.

When the shudders of her orgasm stopped, Giorgio stayed buried deep in her. Maddie held his head, pulling him to her she ran her small, pink tongue along his bottom lip. He angled his mouth over her sensuous lips and sucked her tongue into his mouth. Her inner muscles squeezed him.

He groaned, "I—"

"Shh, no talking. Kissing and sex," she whispered, "lots of sex."

He smiled down into those moss-green eyes and thrust into her heat. Thrust after thrust into her, he kissed her wherever he was able to reach while she begged him to go faster, harder. The ripples of her orgasm drove him to another powerful climax as he thrust himself to the hilt, shuddering in his own fireball of bliss. He held his weight off Maddie.

Giorgio caressed her damp hair, pushing the silky mass away from her flushed face and finding her lips parted. He placed a gentle kiss on their sweetness. Holding her siren's body to him, her scent—sex and jasmine—filled his head. *I'm going to have the landscaper add jasmine to the garden.*

He must have dozed. When Giorgio stirred, she was still

in his arms, her fingers stroking the hair on his chest. He held her, and she moved to lay on top of him.

"Hungry?" Giorgio asked.

"Only for more of this… can you?"

"Oh, a challenge," he growled and nibbled on her neck. "Well, for you, I can go all night."

"Good. Since it's only around eleven in the morning, I accept."

He kissed her, a long, slow one, exploring the contours of her mouth. He whispered, "Come with me."

Her body moved on him again as she said, "I thought I just did, and more than once."

He smiled as his hands massaged the two globes of her pert, toned buttocks. "I thought we could take a bath… but right here in bed is good. Then, we can go play in the tub."

He reached for another condom, amazed at how ready he was for this temptress.

He lay back propped against the pillows. She moaned and lifted herself off him long enough for Giorgio to roll on a fresh condom. Then she held him in her small hand. Maddie raised herself up enough to guide him to the heat of her entrance. She lowered herself an inch at a time down his length. Her heat surrounded him, as he slipped into her. She held his cheeks, rubbing one thumb along his bottom lip, and guided his mouth to her breast.

"Do that thing you did before." Her voice was a soft caress.

Giorgio kissed her breast and then sucked her swollen nipple into his mouth, lathing the bud with his tongue. His hand skimmed over her abdomen, and his finger slipped into her wet heat.

"Yes, that." Maddie moved her hips, rocking back and forth on Giorgio. "You feel

sooo good in me," she groaned. "Oh, oh… ahh." She tightened her inner muscles, driving him wild, and in a matter of moments, they both climaxed in shuddering waves of release.

Giorgio scooted down on the bed, pulling her along to lay across his upper body. He kissed her damp neck, loving the feel of her breasts against his chest as she clung to him. She sighed, and Giorgio thought he had never heard a better sound.

CHAPTER 4

The late-afternoon sun filtered through the sheer curtains of Giorgio's bedroom, casting shadows around the room. Maddie stirred in his strong arms, and Giorgio rolled over, giving her a brief kiss before he got up from the bed. She couldn't help but admire his sun-bronzed back covered in rippling muscles. His butt looked as if it were carved from granite as he walked naked into the bathroom.

He wasn't gone too long but sadly, when he returned, his hair was damp. He'd put on a pair of well-worn, faded jeans and a light-blue t-shirt that molded to his broad chest, hinting at the washboard muscles of his abdomen. The short sleeves of his shirt stretched around his biceps. Maddie had wanted to see him in all his glorious nakedness... dripping wet.

"The shower is all yours. I'm going to get us something to eat."

She felt confused and hurt. *Is Giorgio finished? I'm not.* "Oh... okay... I..."

Giorgio must have heard the dejection in her voice. Barefoot, he sauntered over to the bed and reached for her, pulling her naked body to him. His hand slid down her back, cupping her buttock, dragging her into his hard body.

"No clothes here. I put these on," he chuckled, "because I don't want to frighten Maria, while I get us lunch." He brushed his lips across her temple.

"Lunch?"

"Yes. Food for strength. You know." He winked.

The glint in his aqua eyes heated Maddie's cheeks. Giorgio kissed her lips and brushed a gentle kiss on her nose. His tender touch grasped her hand and held her palm to the crotch of his jeans. She felt his hard length and couldn't help rubbing her hand on him.

He pulled away. "*Strega,* you are a witch."

He walked out of his bedroom, whistling a tune. Maddie stretched on the bed then padded to the bathroom, walking on the heated marble floor past the sunken tub, and moved toward the glass-enclosed shower. A heated towel rack stood near the shower and next to that, the control pad for the rainfall function. She pressed the pad and selected a comfortable temperature for the water, then showered. By the time Giorgio came back, she had wrapped a towel around herself and dried her hair.

He balanced a tray with food on his forearm and hand. In his other hand, he held her clothes, and her stiletto heels hung from two of his long fingers. She walked over and took her clothes from him. "Thanks."

"I gave Maria the rest of the day off."

Maddie felt the heat rise into her cheeks. "Did she see my clothes?" she asked as she set them down on an accent chair near the fireplace, placing her shoes on the floor next to the chair.

"No," Giorgio said his mouth twitching with amusement.

She giggled. "Liar."

He laughed and said, "Who do you think folded your clothes? Why don't we eat in the sitting room?"

For the briefest of moments, Maddie wondered if this was the norm for Maria to fold his other women's clothes. "Let me put my blouse on."

He stopped walking and looked at her. With a devilish glint in his gaze, he said, "No, just keep the towel on."

Giorgio set the tray on the coffee table in front of a long, blue-leather couch. Then he opened a bottle of wine. "We can eat here."

They sat on the floor of his sitting room on a Persian rug in the same shades of blues and cream colors of the bedroom suite. They leaned against the sofa with their legs stretched out in front of them. Giorgio handed her a glass of wine. She nibbled on a wedge of provolone and then sipped the ruby-red liquid.

"Here, try this." Giorgio handed Maddie a breadstick wrapped with a slice of prosciutto.

She took a bite. "Oh, this is delicious. What is it?"

"A type of ham. The best comes from Parma, up north on the mainland." He kissed her neck and bare shoulder.

"I've never had anything this delicious."

"Neither have I," he said against her skin.

She backed away. "Are you teasing me?"

"No, never," Giorgio said as he dragged her across his lap.

Her towel fell away, and Giorgio kissed her lips, tasting the wine on her small, pink tongue. Kissing the corner of her mouth then her delicate jaw. He moved to her neck. His lips lingered. He couldn't get enough of her satin-smooth skin while he kissed her shoulder, his hands stroking her breasts. He plucked a nipple into a hard bud before moving on.

She reached her small hand down his t-shirt-clad chest, drifting lower to his jeans. He lightly nipped at her nipple.

"Yes, I like that," she said as she tried to unzip his pants.

"Now, I want *my* dessert," he said.

She stopped and looked at him. His hands slid to the curve of her waist and lifted her onto the edge of the leather sofa cushion. He knelt in front of Maddie and reached his hand into the mass of silky hair at her nape, cupping her slender neck. Giorgio brought her lips to his for a long, sizzling kiss.

He dragged his lips to the smooth skin of her neck, feeling the pulse beat, then he moved to her collarbone, and the hollow between. He dipped his tongue into that hollow before licking and kissing his way to the valley of her breasts. She sighed as he kissed the underside of a breast. He kissed the satin-soft skin covering her ribs.

"Lean against the sofa back," he said after the last kiss he placed on her belly.

Then he spread her shapely legs, and his hands reached around her knees as he wedged his shoulders between her open thighs. Her blonde curls were damp and beckoning him. Giorgio had dreamed of this moment—sinking his tongue into her. She tasted better than he'd thought possible.

His gaze caught hers. "All wet for me. You taste like heaven."

Maddie's eyelids slid down over her moss-green eyes, and Giorgio licked into her pink center, inhaling her scent. He used the flat of his tongue to lick up to her exposed clit. Touching that berry-like pink flesh with the tip of his tongue and then sliding back into her center. His thumbs opened her wider to sheath his tongue into her core.

Maddie arched her body and called his name. Giorgio thrust his tongue in and out, in and out. He licked back up to her clit, moving her spread legs, so her thighs rested on his shoulders. Giorgio kissed the smooth skin of her inner thigh, feeling the muscle quiver under his lips.

"G… Giorgio…"

He held Maddie, spread before him, sending his tongue in to circle the glistening bud. She raised her knees off his shoulders, offering herself to his mouth. Giorgio slid a finger into her wet heat, sliding in and out.

"Yes, yes, oh God, yes," she moaned.

Then he slid a second finger into her vagina, finding the spot to give her the most pleasure. He curved his fingers to stroke her slowly on her G-spot while the tip of his tongue played with her clit.

Her breath came in soft pants, then she moved her hips, taking his fingers into her. Her breath grew rapid and louder. She cried then gasped as she pulsed around his fingers. Her hands brushed his hair, holding him to her. The heels of her feet pressing on his shoulders as her orgasm pulsated. He couldn't resist sucking her clit and crooking his fingers once more.

"So good, ahh," she yelled.

Maddie shuddered, rolling her hips. Giorgio smiled, and then slowly, he thrust deeper into her heat as his tongue slipped over her clit.

She gasped, "Oh, you're going to make me come again."

He didn't answer her. He nibbled very lightly on her clit and then pressed his tongue from the base to the tip of that berry before circling and sucking her clit. His fingers slowly slid deeper into her center. Again, he crooked them, and her body arched off the sofa cushion. He felt the pulsations of her third orgasm just before Maddie screamed her pleasure. She held his head to her, stroking his hair, and he inhaled her scent.

MADDIE COULDN'T MOVE. He gave her the best orgasm ever. Sex with him was the best she had ever had. Now, all she wanted to do was to give *him* pleasure, but her body was a puddle of satiated bliss.

Giorgio's cell phone rang. He groaned, "I should get that. You stay put; we aren't finished." He rose from his knees and walked to the nightstand by his bed. "Pronto," he said into the phone.

She guessed Italian for hello. Maddie stood and walked over to get her blouse. Giorgio, with the phone still to his ear, walked over and shook his head. He ended the call with some *ciaos*, then slid his arms around Maddie's waist, kissing her brow before he said, "That was my attorney. Your father confirmed receipt of the money, and my vintner is already on his way to California."

"Perfect. I'll make arrangements for a flight home."

He held her to him. "Why not stay for a few days?" His big hands slid down her back, pulling her to him and squeezing her butt. "Let me show you Sicily as only a Sicilian can." The bulge of his erection pressed into her. "Then you go back to LA… and I go to work."

It was such a tempting offer to spend time with Giorgio, have fun, more mind-blowing sex, and then go home. Maddie thought for a moment, *why not,* and said, "Yes, I would like that very much… or at least… until I get this…" Her hungry fingers went into the waistband of his denim jeans, and she stroked his hard flesh. "In me."

Giorgio smiled as he unzipped his fly and pushed down his jeans, stepping out of them. Maddie knelt before him, her fingers closed over his hard length, and her tongue touched the tip.

Caressing her shoulders, he lifted her to her feet. Then he sighed, "Soon, but there is no time for that… or to get to the bed."

"Wait! A—I'm not on—"

"Ah! *Si*, you are correct, protection." He went to his nightstand and then came back to her. His hands went around her waist and slid down to cup her buttocks. He kissed her lips, and his tongue snaked into her mouth as she wiggled her butt in his big hands, secure in the knowledge he could hold her without a wall to lean against. His feet were planted apart, and he bent his knees, lifted her, and impaled Maddie on his oh-so-huge cock. She stretched and melted around him as he filled her.

"Oh, yes." Maddie gave as good as she got as his mouth hungrily devoured hers. She wrapped her legs around his narrow waist, locking her ankles, holding his dark, stubble-covered cheeks as she gave up her mouth to his demanding lips.

His big hands held her, lifting and lowering her onto his magnificent male length as if she weighed nothing. Maddie pulled her mouth from his to take in gulps of air. She saw his brilliant smile as he thrust in and out faster and faster. Holding onto his shoulders, her head fell back, and his lips pressed kisses on her exposed neck. They were both damp from the exquisite exertion. Maddie moaned, and a gasp escaped her half-parted lips.

"Come for me," Giorgio whispered.

"Yes, oh… so good," she moaned.

They came together in shared bliss. Her legs trembled as they slid down his body. He bent and caught her behind her knees, cradling her to him. She looped her arms around his neck, resting her head against his chest. Feeling the pounding of his heart, she closed her eyes. Giorgio walked to the bed and laid her on the cool sheets. The bed dipped as he lay, tugging her back to his chest. He tucked his knees under hers and draped an arm across her waist. She melted against him, and they both fell asleep.

Maddie woke up and glanced over to the nightstand to

see the time. She calculated that it was early morning in LA. Giorgio leaned over, kissing her shoulder.

She snuggled against him before she said, "I have to get my phone. I left it downstairs. I want to text my PA and let her know I'm staying on for a few days."

He rolled out of bed. "Here, wear this," he said, tossing her his button-down shirt.

She giggled as she caught it. Shoving her arms into the overly long sleeves, the shirt came down past her knees. His cologne clung to the fabric, cocooning her in his scent.

The villa was in semi-darkness, but she could see where she was going. Maddie padded barefoot down the three flights of stairs to the living room. It was the last place she'd had her purse and phone—she smiled, remembering how she stripped for him and how that led to a marathon of the best sex she'd ever had.

Giorgio exceeded her wildest dreams. Standing in the middle of his bedroom having sex. She had never done that before. She finished her text, then turned off her phone. She put it back into her purse, taking it with her as she went back up the stairs. When Maddie reached Giorgio's bedroom, she found him in the bathroom. He'd filled the sunken bathtub. She slid his shirt off and stepped down into the warm water of the enormous whirlpool where he waited for her. On the side of the tub, a bottle of wine and one glass sat on a tray.

"Only *one* glass?" she asked.

"You'll like it, I promise," he said in his slight Italian accent as he poured the wine into the glass.

He drank some and kissed her, sending wine into her mouth. "Later, I will drink some off your body."

Taking another sip, he kissed her. Now, she understood the game. Maddie slid her tongue into his waiting mouth, swirling her tongue around his.

"Your turn," she said, taking a sip of the ruby-red wine.

They played at that game until the bath water got cold, and half the bottle of wine was gone. Giorgio lifted her out of the tub. She reached for a towel to wrap around her hair and then dried herself with a large, fluffy bath towel.

"Don't forget the wine. I have an idea," she said over her shoulder.

Giorgio dried his body, and taking the bottle, went to the bed.

"You lay down now; it's my turn to play." She giggled and left the towel on the floor, keeping the other wrapped on her hair.

He did precisely what Maddie wanted. He reclined, resting his broad shoulders against the massive wood-carved headboard, raising his arms to interlace his fingers behind his head. His athletic body honed with muscles and a smattering of dark hair across his chest that became a thin line over his abdomen. He spread his muscle-covered legs. His long, huge erection—the prize—waited for her to do what she had wanted.

Maddie crawled up the bed, so hot for him. All she wanted was to take as much of him as she could into her mouth. A zing of excitement shot into her core. She stopped long enough to pull the towel from her hair, shaking her head and letting the damp strands fall around her. Giorgio was a fantasy come to life, so virile and now, she would do what he had stopped her from doing earlier. She slid her hands along his legs, from his knees to his upper thighs, digging her fingers into his muscles, feeling his power and strength. She smiled up at him, and he held her gaze in his aqua eyes, as she tugged on a corner of her lower lip.

He groaned, "You're going to kill me. I can tell."

"I hope not." She smiled.

Maddie didn't give Giorgio a chance to say more as she bent her head and ran her tongue along the length of him.

Taking the velvety smooth tip into her mouth, Maddie swirled her tongue around the head, tasting his excitement. She moved to take a little more of his beautiful erection into her mouth. Holding his shaft in one hand, her fingers unable to close around the base, she slid her mouth up, kissing his engorged head. She slid her tongue on the underside to tease along the ridge. Each time she took more of his length into her mouth, stroking the underside with her tongue, she heard him groan. Maddie cupped Giorgio's balls with one hand while she flicked her tongue over the velvet-soft head, stroking his shaft with her other hand up and down his length, each time her tongue lingered under the head.

"Strega," he said while his fingers dug into her hair, holding her.

She took him down her throat. Then his body bucked. Maddie sucked harder, taking him deep, loving the power she had over him.

"Ahh… Ahh, strega," he shouted.

She smiled around him, swallowing as spurts of his cum flowed down her throat. When he relaxed, she sucked again.

"Ahh, you *do* want to kill me." He touched her hair in a caress, then lifted her. "Come here." He held her against his side and kissed her mouth. "Will you stay in my arms tonight?"

Maddie rested her head on his shoulder and enjoyed being held in Giorgio's arms. She was going to break her number-one rule. She hadn't slept the whole night with a man in five years.

CHAPTER 5

The next morning when they woke up, she and Giorgio showered and then went downstairs to the kitchen. Giorgio prepared breakfast, espresso, and a sweet roll he'd called a *cornetto*. It reminded Maddie of a brioche, but when she bit into the flaky pastry, her eyes rounded as her tongue tasted the chocolate cream in the center.

"OMG," Maddie moaned. "My new breakfast choice. These are delicious."

He laughed. "You sound the same as when you come." She felt a blush stain her cheeks but didn't reply.

"There are so many beautiful places in Sicily."

Mmm," she moaned, reaching for Giorgio.

"Pay attention," he joked. "I think you'll like Erice. It's a medieval town built around the 1100s. Then we can go to Marsala—"

"Like the wine?" she asked.

"Exactly, that is where it is produced. I have a friend who owns a bed and breakfast in Erice, so if you want, I can call him and let him know we would like to spend the night there."

"I think it will be fun, but first, can we stop at a boutique where I can get a casual outfit or two?"

"Yes, I know just the place. Are you ready?"

He took his Lamborghini from the garage, and they drove into Palermo, stopping at a boutique. Maddie bought a yellow-eyelet summer dress and a pair of low-heeled sandals. She bought a hand-painted silk scarf and a few other items of clothing. The sales associate pointed out some fun tortoiseshell statement earrings and three stacking tortoise-shell bangles. Maddie held the earrings to her ears and looked in the mirror on the display case.

"Okay, I'll take them," she said.

Then in the dressing room, Maddie changed into the eyelet summer dress, taking her diamond-stud earrings off and placing them along with her gold wristwatch into the jewelry pouch of her purse.

Giorgio had wanted to pay for the clothes, but Maddie wouldn't allow that. When she walked out of the dressing room, he joked about how she looked like a well-loved Italian model in her street clothes and her flowing blonde hair. He pulled her into him for a kiss. Maddie took out her phone and snapped a picture of them.

Then he drove on the highway along the Sicilian coast for about an hour and a half to Trapani. Maddie had used her phone to search information on Erice. "Will we take the *funivia* to the town?" She smiled at him, happy by his look of surprise at her knowing the Italian name for the sky lift.

"Is that what you have been doing on your phone? Research. No, we will drive to the top of the mountain and keep the car at my friend's B&B."

Once off the autostrada, they were on a narrow, two-lane road, driving up the mountain. The only barrier on the side of the road was a low stone wall. Giorgio drove the Lamborghini higher and higher up the mountain to the medieval town of Erice which laid high above the city of Trapani. By the time they'd arrived at the medieval town, it was *pranzo*, so Giorgio parked the Lamborghini at the B&B, and they walked to the restaurant owned by another of his friends.

After lunch, they sat and talked with Giorgio's childhood friend Gustavo. "Gus for short," he said to Maddie as he introduced his wife Sara to her. Giorgio and Maddie sat with Gus and Sara, all enjoying a wonderful meal of homemade pasta with a fresh basil sauce, grilled fish, and vegetables.

Gus and Sara both spoke English, although Sara wasn't as fluent as Gustavo. Gus told Maddie about how he and Giorgio had both gone to Harvard University. "After undergrad, I wanted to come back to Sicily and open a chain of restaurants. In reality, I wanted to come back and marry Sara. I was afraid she wouldn't wait for me."

Sara said, "He was right to come home."

Gus told Maddie about all the fun he and Giorgio had discovering hamburgers, hot dogs, and baseball. How on the spur of the moment over summer break, they both bought motorcycles and rode cross country, stopping along the way to see the Grand Canyon and the Pacific Ocean.

"Giorgio always wanted to have a big wine business, so he went on to grad school. I was happy to come home and marry the love of my life."

Maddie's heart clenched as she watched Gus pull Sara onto his lap and cradle her six-month-pregnant belly as he kissed her cheek.

"Now, we buy all our wine from Giorgio," Sara said.

Giorgio joked with his friend, saying, "You have a wonderful wife, and you are fortunate that she lets you ramble on. But now, we have to go."

"Thank you for a fabulous meal and the interesting stories," Maddie said.

She and Giorgio walked along the cobbled streets, past shops that were now closed for the afternoon. He tugged her closer to him, and they held hands on the way back to the bed and breakfast.

"Are we going to do that, resting thing?" Maddie asked.

His brows drew together. "*Riposo?*" He laughed then said, "Oh, you want to sleep?" He hugged her to him.

She felt the heat rise into her cheeks before she looked away.

"Your blushes are the same as when I make you come." Giorgio smiled. "Oh, no. Your cheeks got redder."

She lifted her chin, peering down her nose, pretending to hold an *I'm better than that* attitude. "No teasing allowed. I'm trying to learn the customs."

He pulled her into his arms and kissed her brow. "I am happy to teach you… *all* my customs."

Walking down the narrow-cobbled streets, he'd meshed his longer fingers with hers as they strolled the few blocks to the hotel. Giorgio took her around to the back, and they climbed the outer steps of the old stone building to their room. Maddie was never one to be shy, but now she hesitated. Giorgio took her hand and led her into the bathroom. It was nothing like the one in his master bedroom at his home. Or even the one in her guest bedroom at his villa. This was tiny and efficient. Giorgio did though manage to get her into the shower with him. He soaped her and then rinsed every part of her.

When she tried to do the same for him, Giorgio stopped her, pulling her soaking wet from the shower, leaving a puddle on the tile floor. He held open a big, fluffy towel and with soft strokes over her body, he dried her. With the same towel, he briskly dried himself. She walked to the bed, but taking her hand, Giorgio led her to a comfortable-looking, upholstered armchair.

"Sit here for me," he coaxed.

She slowly lowered herself onto the seat. Giorgio knelt in front of her and spread her knees apart. She slid down on the cushion.

"You are exquisite," he whispered. "I have wanted to do this all day… Have *my* dessert."

He kissed her lips, sucking her bottom lip into his mouth, running his tongue over it, then kissing her jaw and down her neck. He took his sweet time on her breasts, kissing and exciting her nipples. When he kissed her stomach, a zap of heat went through Maddie as desire seeped into her core, wetting her. She couldn't hold back the moan of sheer pleasure as he slid his tongue from her belly button on a path down over her abdomen to the center of her spread legs.

His aqua eyes held hers as his lips brushed Maddie's curls. She reached her fingers into the thickness of his short dark hair. She loved what he did and was so grateful that he liked doing this very intimate act with her. Giorgio was a great lover, willing to let her explore him and his very well-hidden, bad-boy side.

"You taste so good on my tongue," he said with his lips against her curls.

Maddie slid lower onto the cushion and rested her shoulders against the back of the chair. Giorgio lifted her legs over the padded arms of the accent chair, his big hands rough from the grapevines. When she'd commented about his calluses, he'd said, "I may have custom-made Armani suits and my own jet, but I am a hands-on type of guy—" Then he proceeded to show her. Now his mouth brought her to the brink of release. And then he stopped.

She looked into his deep-aqua eyes, the gold flecks burning into her. "Giorgio," she panted.

"What do you want?" he asked.

She squirmed on the edge of the cushion. Giorgio held her legs in place over the arms of the chair.

"Tell me," he said, gazing into her eyes, and then his lips brushed her center.

"Oh," she whimpered, "I want you to finish what you started."

"Tell me exactly."

Her breath hitched. "I want you to put your tongue in me and—"

"Lick you."

"Oh… yes… that too," she panted.

"Your cheeks are as pink as your glistening folds," he said, and then he did lick her. Sucking on her clit, bringing her back to a fever pitch of excitement. His handsome face, between her legs, what his mouth did to her. She couldn't think anymore—just feel.

"Oh, God, make me come. Yes, oh yes, yes." Maddie gasped, unable to say another word.

Giorgio spread her and thrust his tongue deep into her, licking up to her clit. As soon as his tongue ran along the most sensitive part of her clitoris, once, twice, she exploded into shattering bliss. She came against his tongue in shuddering waves of pleasure.

Giorgio slid two of his long fingers into her pulsating vagina and sucked her clit into his mouth. His lips… were entirely around the base, suck, suck, then he was lashing at her oh-so-sensitive clit with his tongue. "Oh God," she moaned. She'd never experienced anything like what he was doing.

"Oh, I love it," she said as her body arched, mindless to what she was saying.

His fingers found her spot, slowly stroking. "Ahhh, yes. I…

I'm coming again, ahh." Her legs lifted off the arms of the chair, her thighs quivered as they clasped his head. She climaxed in blissful waves of release. She held his head to her until the last shudders of her orgasm stopped. She was mindless.

Giorgio kept his amazing mouth on her. When she recovered and her breathing returned to normal, he picked her up and walked from the chair to stand Maddie beside the bed. He nuzzled her ear and whispered, "Lay down on your stomach."

She moaned, "Oh Giorgio, I don't—"

"I know you'll like what I have in mind."

She did as he asked. Giorgio spread her legs, massaging her buttocks, stroking up her spine to her shoulder blades, and back down to her buttocks. Then he pressed her hips up, lifting her. Maddie scooted to her knees and felt the head of his massive erection touch her vagina. She moaned and pushed back, taking him into her body.

"Yes, like that, *Maddalena mia*, see how nice this feels?"

"Yes, so good. Ahh, ahh," she couldn't talk as he pistoned into her.

Maddie pushed back, and Giorgio thrust deeper. He reached around her and massaged her clit. She spread her knees wider and arched her spine, lifting her buttocks. She was panting as Giorgio went into her, then a long moan escaped her. He thrust faster, rubbing her clit, and she exploded into ecstasy. Her spasms clenched around him, and he stayed in her until the orgasm ended.

Giorgio leaned over and brushed the hair from her neck. "More?" he asked as he kissed the spot under her ear.

All she could do was sigh. "Yes… more. Have I told you how good you feel? So big."

"Your orgasms tell me." Giorgio smiled.

He held her to him and stroke after deep stroke, she cried

out her pleasure. Then he rolled onto his back. "Here, like this. Straddle me but face away."

She eagerly did, and then he held her hips as she lowered herself onto his erection. He reached around, and his fingers plucked her nipples as she rode him in this new position. She didn't have time to think as the coil in her belly unwound into another explosive orgasm, stroking him into her core. He groaned and pumped up into her; they came together in a mass of shuddering pleasure.

Giorgio turned Maddie to face him. She was limp as a rag doll as she stretched out on top of him in the circle of his strong, capable arms. Her head rested on his chest, and she said, "Your heart is racing the same as mine."

Gradually, as their heartbeats slowed, she closed her eyes, her fingers stroking his jaw.

GIORGIO WAS content to hold Madeline Watson in his arms. He knew the moment she fell asleep, laying on top of him with the soft curves of her sated body molded to his. Giorgio stroked his hand along her body, holding her sleeping form to him. He realized she'd never made love in either of those positions—a smile tugged at the corner of his lips. He had so much more he would teach her before the short time they had would be over.

With a grin on his lips and the scent of Maddie surrounding him, he closed his eyes. She stirred in his arms, and he held her tighter. She kissed his chest.

"I really like *riposo*," she murmured against his skin.

He brushed a strand of her silky blonde hair from her face. "Me too," he whispered.

They dosed for a while. When he woke, he felt her move

against him, and he kissed the top of her head, breathing in her scent.

"Are you ready to go dancing?" he asked.

"I love to dance," she said as she rolled over. Her eyes were closed as she smiled; her lips kiss swollen.

He couldn't help but run his hand along the curve of her hip. Then she sat up and got out of bed. Walking over to his clothes, she picked up his t-shirt and slipped it over her head. Pulling her blonde hair out of the shirt, she let it fall down her back. Giorgio slipped on his boxers. Then Maddie walked to the French doors of the balcony.

"Oh, look at this! We're above the clouds," Maddie said.

Giorgio walked over and stood behind her, placing his hands on her shoulders. She was so petite, he was able to rest his chin on the top of her head. His arms moved around her waist, snuggling her against him.

"I love this sight," Giorgio said. "When the clouds roll in, we can look down on them. It doesn't always happen, but it does more so at this time of year."

"This is amazing. Erice is above the clouds."

She leaned into him, her hands caressing his forearms, her fingers drawing patterns. That was all she did, and his blood raced through him. He had the beginning of an erection.

"Mmm, that feels nice," Maddie said as she wiggled her bottom against him.

He playfully smacked her butt. "Let's save some for later."

"Aw, spoilsport. Have I tuckered you out?" She giggled.

"Now, you'll pay for that, *strega*. You won't have *any* sleep tonight. But let's get dressed and go out. Gus said that there will be dancing tonight in the *piazza*."

"In the square? Outside?"

"Yes, like the other night." They went to another restaurant for dinner. After dinner, they walked along the medieval streets of the ancient town. She had said that the magic of being above the clouds added to the charm and beauty of Erice.

"Ah listen, the musicians are tuning their instruments. They will be starting soon," Giorgio said.

"What do they play?"

"Salsa and upbeat music. I know you can line dance; I should have asked if you can salsa?"

Maddie shimmied her shoulders and swung her hips. "Yes, and some other dances too."

He didn't want to keep her out too late. He wanted to get her back to their room and make good on his promise of keeping her up all night.

In the morning, Giorgio brought coffee and *cornetti* up to their room. She'd said the pastry was her *new* favorite breakfast, and he happily indulged her. They sat on the balcony eating.

"This view is breathtaking." Giorgio looked up at Maddie, her cheeks held a blush from their night of passion.

"Yes, it is truly beautiful." His gaze lingered on her before he glanced at the view, "It is spectacular, with Trapani and the Egadi Islands, in the distance.

After breakfast, Maddie dressed in one of the outfits she'd bought at the boutique in Palermo. Beige linen pants with a pink blouse, she pulled her hair back from her face with a headband and put on the earrings and bangles she'd bought. Slipping into a pair of low-heel sandals, Maddie was ready.

They drove back down the mountain to the seacoast town of Marsala. Giorgio parked his matte-black Lamborghini, and then they strolled along the streets of the tiny village. Giorgio watched her as she smothered a yawn. He laughed when he realized she tried to hide it from him.

"Too much dancing?" Giorgio asked.

"You know that's not it." She rose on her toes and whispered into his ear, "It was after."

He held back a chuckle as he said, "Oh… yes. I remember. You haven't slept all night." He liked the way she ignored him, lifting her chin. "Tell me about the windmills, oh great fountain of knowledge."

He couldn't hold back his laugh as he said, "I am sorry if this sounds like a history lesson."

"No, Giorgio, I'm interested. Tell me about the windmills and the salt production."

"The windmills with their red roofs were first used in medieval times to pump water out of the salt pans as they make sea salt. Sicily's climate is very much like southern California," Giorgio said.

"Or SoCal, as we say." Maddie smiled. "I never realized how similar. Or the rich history of this beautiful island."

"If you stayed longer, I would take you to Taormina to see the ancient Greek and Roman theater."

She sighed. "I have to go… home."

After *pranzo* on the way back to his villa, they stopped at Segesta. Maddie had asked about the ancient site she spotted as they drove. Giorgio took the off ramp and parked his Lamborghini in the parking lot where there were a handful of other cars. The weather was warm, and some other tourists walked around the ruin. Giorgio told Maddie about the temple.

"It was never finished. There isn't any roof, and the columns were never fluted. They believe it was built around 450 BC. In the spring, the wildflowers in the surrounding fields blossom, turning everything golden."

"It must be beautiful at that time."

When they arrived back at the villa, they walked up the stairs to his bedroom. "Maria left us some food. I'll get a bottle of wine."

"I'm not hungry, but the wine… and… maybe…"

He watched as a blush stained her cheeks, and he said, "A relaxing bath with me."

She bit her bottom lip and then said, "So you can read minds."

"Only yours because we think alike." He kissed her. "What time is your flight tomorrow?"

He didn't know how Maddie felt. She had said she only wanted sex, and at the beginning, that was all he wanted. Then, something happened, and now, maybe he wanted more than sex.

In the morning, they made the sweetest love. Giorgio wanted to memorize her.

Maddie's finger traced his lips, then she sighed into his neck, "I'll never forget you or this time we shared. Every time I have a glass of wine, I will remember you. My very own winemaker."

He held her tighter to his chest, breathing in her jasmine scent. "We had better get dressed, so you don't miss your flight." He paused for a moment, then looked into her eyes. "The offer still stands; I will have my jet take you home."

Maddie shook her head. "No. I'll take the commercial flight my PA booked for me."

"As you wish, *Maddalena mia.*"

Her brows furrowed.

"It means mine. My Madeline. That is what you'll always be."

Maddie lifted her parted lips to his. She murmured, "Well, maybe one more time before I have to go."

HER CHEEKS WERE pink from this last orgasm. She looped her

arms around his neck and whispered, "Now I really do have to rush so I don't miss my flight."

She went back to the guest bedroom to dress while Giorgio dressed in his. A little while later, he knocked on her bedroom door.

"Come in," Maddie said.

She stood next to her suitcase when he entered. Her mass of blonde hair was tied back from her beautiful face. Maddie wore a crisp white blouse with her black pencil skirt and matching blazer; her black stilettos were back on her dainty feet. The transformation was complete. Madeline Watson was once again the bank executive he had first met. He could see that the tough girl was back.

He drove her to the airport and walked beside her to the gate. The air full of the distinct smell of jet fuel. The way she rolled her designer bag screamed, don't touch. The romance had ended.

He was so well known in Palermo and all of Italy. There would be no problem allowing him to accompany Maddie on the tarmac and up the steps to the entrance of the plane. He could have boarded if he wanted to. But Maddie insisted otherwise. She turned to him; he saw the way her lower lip quivered as she looked into his eyes. Did he see sadness?

Then she smiled and put out her hand. "Thank you for *everything,* Mr. Lombardo."

He understood; there were people around, so he gave a slight nod as he said, "You are welcome, Ms. Watson. If I'm ever in LA, I will be sure to look you up."

She whispered in her husky little voice, "I promise to take you sightseeing the same as you did for me."

"I accept." *The challenge.*

CHAPTER 6

Maddie thought of those two words all the way home. He wanted to see her again. By the time the plane landed at LAX, and she got into her car, she was back to the old Maddie. The realist who knew she'd had the best sex ever. But that's all it was. Sex. Men lied and used you for their own gain. Best girlfriends betrayed your trust. No BFFs and no serious boyfriends. She had been gullible, but not anymore. She was strong and capable. Invincible.

Maddie knew that should Giorgio ever come to LA, she would certainly like more of him, but she could go without the mind-blowing sex. *Who am I kidding?* The handsome Sicilian winemaker left his mark on her, and she *knew* it. But fight it, she would. The workaholic who thought of nothing but business and the next deal for her client's financial port-folio was back in charge. She was the barracuda once again.

That night, her phone pinged with a text. Maddie glanced at the number on the screen and recognized the country code—Italy. A warm glow spread through her.

I hope you are home safe and sound.

With a smile on her lips, she texted back. Yes. Thanks.

Then she put her phone on silence and went to take a hot bath, wondering if she would suffer from jet lag.

The following morning, when Maddie arrived at work, the bank looked as busy as ever. The entire first floor of the white, five-story building on the corner of Wilshire Boulevard and Ocean Avenue was devoted to bank customers. Six tellers stood at their stations, three were busy with customers. The assistant manager was at his desk, and Maddie waved to him. She walked over to the bank manager, who'd recently been promoted from her previous position as assistant manager.

"Hi, I just wanted to say congratulations on your promotion. If you're free today, I'd like to take you to lunch."

"Why, thank you. I would like that very much, Ms. Watson."

"Is one o'clock good for you?"

"Yes, see you then."

Maddie took the elevator to the top floor of the building. The door swooshed open, and she walked down the corridor to her corner office. Traci, Maddie's PA, looked up from her desk. Traci could have been a super model, tall and willowy thin with long black hair and brown eyes.

"Good morning, Traci, I brought coffee for us. Why don't you come into my office?"

"Thanks, I'll get my notes so I can update you on the most pressing business."

They drank their coffee while going over the financials of one client. Then Traci went back to her desk.

Giorgio was on Maddie's mind all day—no jet lag—but she'd had a terrible night tossing and turning, thinking of him. At one point, she'd reached over before realizing she was home and alone in her empty bed. Forcing the sexy winemaker from her thoughts, she looked out her office window at the Pacific Ocean. Today, the ocean reminded

Maddie of his eyes. *Did the Pacific always have that hint of aqua in the deep-blue depths?*

She sighed, groaned, and turned from the window. Maddie shook her head. Walking to her desk, she sat and glanced at the file on her computer. *Lombardo Wines. Why is that file open?* Exiting the screen, she scrolled down the list of her clients until she found the one she was searching for. Clicking on the name, she opened the portfolio.

Maddie knew she would have to fly to Tokyo next week to pack the last of her belongings. She glanced at her wrist-watch and caught herself wondering what time it was in Palermo. *Okay, calm down. Focus! Don't get crazy about these thoughts. He's just a guy.* She sighed. *Yes, but what a hunky, sexy man. When he—*She shoved away from her desk and paced the length of her corner office.

With windows on two walls, she had a fantastic view of Wilshire Boulevard and Ocean Avenue in Santa Monica. On the street below, cars whizzed by. A park ran along Ocean Avenue and past the lush green grass, and palm trees was the Pacific Coast Highway, and the Pacific Ocean beyond. A knock on Maddie's door interrupted her thoughts and without permission, Doug, her former fiancé, walked in.

"You," Maddie snapped.

At one time, his sandy-blond hair and whiskey-brown eyes were all she longed for. He sauntered over to where she stood. She realized that in her stilettos, he was only an inch taller than she.

"Hi, beautiful. I waited until your watchdog stepped away from her desk."

"Don't talk about Traci like that." Maddie didn't even try to be civil or keep the anger from her voice. "What do you want?"

"I need to talk to you. Come to lunch with me."

"No."

"I—"

"What is this urgent matter? There isn't any reason for you and me to talk. You're in legal, and I'm *now* in finance."

He was the reason she'd transferred out of loss mitigation and into finance. The reason why she had accepted a position with an international bank in Tokyo and moved there. Why she'd closed her condo in Malibu and never looked back. She had missed her parents, her brother Michael, her sister-in-law Alison, and their baby, but it had been challenging to remain in LA. *He* was the reason she'd closed her heart to love. Now, he stood in her office.

"Nancy and I are getting a divorce," Doug said matter of fact.

Maddie looked at the man who'd jilted her, rejected her, but, most of all, *humiliated* her. The man she'd once loved. Shrugging a shoulder, she said, "What do you want from me? Sympathy?" She didn't have to work at making her voice cold and indifferent. She no longer had any feelings for him.

"I just—"

Maddie raised her hand. "No. To whatever it is. I'm not interested in anything you have to say. Leave my office and do not, I repeat, *do not* come in here again." She strode to the door of her office and turned the knob to open it.

"No, Mad, don't. Just hear me out. I want—"

She faced him. "Clearly, you have a hearing impairment. I *do not* want to listen to anything you have to say. Furthermore, if it concerns bank business, take it to James. You remember him? He's the other financial advisor." Maddie flung the door open. "Get. Out."

Doug walked toward the open door. "You're being so irrational. As usual," he said, storming past her, flailing his arms in disgust.

Maddie swung the door closed and walked over to her desk. *Am I irrational?* She didn't want to see him or hear anything about his life. Why should she? After all, he dumped her and had no interest in what happened. *He'd turned his back on me and left me to deal with all the cancelations and then to make matters worse, my parents ended up paying for a wedding that never took place. 'I don't love you,' he'd said, among other things, and then he had the audacity to ask me for the airline tickets and our honeymoon itinerary. Why should I care about him?*

The following morning—the day of her wedding—she'd taken his two-karate diamond engagement ring and thrown it into the ocean along with her hopes and dreams of love and a family. She wasn't angry—not even hurt—any longer.

Maddie had walked around in a daze, going over and over Doug's words. Weeks of agony and despair were haunted by his actions and second guessing how she hadn't realized what was going on right under her nose. Friends were treacherous, and Doug turned out to be a shallow man. She learned a difficult lesson, one she'd never repeat. That was the day she'd decided to move to Japan.

Now, here she was five years later, determined to stay in LA. No more running away from feelings or Doug. Her family needed her, and she needed them. She'd missed her mother and father even though they'd made a point of meeting in Hawaii, a great halfway point between Tokyo and LA. They'd get together a few times a year and *always* for Christmas.

Maddie, by choice, didn't have any girlfriends or confidants. Although, there were plenty of men who were just friends and some who had been more. What was she going to do? She was twenty-eight and single. She owned a multi-million-dollar condo on the beach in Malibu. She owned her car, and she had saved and saved, so now what to do?

She was tired and didn't want to continually fly to Japan; she wanted something different, but what? Loss mitigation and finance were all she knew. That had been the reason her father had asked her to fly to Sicily. Her father wanted her to take the position as head of the loss mitigation department again. But that would put her in close contact with Doug, and she didn't want to see him, let alone work with him.

She'd flown to Japan once more to pack the last of her belongings and have them shipped to California. The flight home from Tokyo had been delayed, and Maddie was exhausted by the time she retrieved her car from LAX's long-term parking. It was well past eleven p.m. when Maddie pulled her car into her condo's two-car garage. Then she grabbed her suitcase from the trunk, and taking the interior steps, walked into her entry.

She was greeted by a vase full of red roses, and scattered over the entry floor were red rose petals. Her heart raced with excitement. *Giorgio had come. He found me. He's here.* She left her suitcase and purse in the entry and dropped her jacket over the back of the living room couch. Unbuttoning her blouse on the way, she hurried into her bedroom. Excitement coursing through her veins.

"You!" Her fingers froze on the button. "What are *you* doing here? Get out of my bed. You have no right." Her voice was ice.

"Hey, beautiful," Doug said confidently. "I told you I was getting a divorce and need you back in my life."

"Well, I don't want *you* back in *my* life. Now, get out." The disappointment at not finding Giorgio overwhelmed her, and anger consumed her.

The audacity of Doug to lie naked in her bed. Ooh. She was speechless. Regret that it wasn't Giorgio seeped into her soul.

Maddie stormed out of the bedroom, shouting over her shoulder, "Get out now before I call security."

She made a mental note to call them anyway. "Leave my key on the way out. I can't believe you kept it." She shook with anger.

She was beyond upset that Doug thought she would drop everything and take him back. He wasn't shallow. No, he was an arrogant asshole to think she would go through all the hurt and humiliation again. Tomorrow, she'd have the locks changed and bar him from ever entering her home again.

She ran into her guest bedroom and yanked the bedspread to the foot of the bed. Maddie listened as he stormed down the hall, yelling that she was irrational. He slammed the front door with such force, the house shuddered. Sitting on the edge of the bed, she called the security office. Did she want a locksmith to come now? She decided that tomorrow morning before eight would be fine.

In the morning, she would see about buying new bedroom furniture, definitely a new mattress. Right now, she didn't even want to use the master bathroom. She had to get the odor of Doug out of her home. Maddie showered in the guest bathroom, put on her well-worn cotton nightshirt, and crawled under the covers.

Maddie wanted her old life back, but not with Doug or any deceitful girlfriends. So, she wouldn't get married or have a house full of kids as she'd planned. Life handed her a different existence, a lonely and untrusting one. But one where her heart wouldn't get hurt again. Her jaw clenched with determination. She *would* survive; after all, she was tough.

~

SHE DECIDED to purchase all new furniture for her condo, and her mother's interior designer told Maddie she would rush the job. The designer would need a minimum of two weeks to paint, have new window coverings made, and have the furniture delivered.

Maddie had always been an equestrian and rode every chance she could, so she drove to Santa Barbara and the old stable where she'd ridden growing up. The stable manager asked her if she planned on entering the horse show in Del Mar. Maddie decided that it would be fun and would give her a reason to stay in Santa Barbara. She'd stay there for the two weeks, preparing for the horse show. She rode her horse Sir Prance A Lot every day in preparation.

Maddie fought not to think of the last time she rode in Sicily with Giorgio. She tried not to think of him at all. It was just sex. Okay, the best sex she'd ever had, but only sex, nonetheless. They had agreed to that; she wouldn't change their mutual decision. Anyway, what would she say? *I want more. Oh, yes.*

A smile tugged at her lips. The last time they were together, she'd panted those precise words after her third orgasm. He'd laughed that free-spirited laugh of his and then proceeded to give her exactly what she wanted and needed. He was so good at what he did to her. Her nipples tightened, and a sweet burn pulsed between her legs. *Stop that.* Sir Prance A Lot snickered and shied away.

"Sorry, fella, my mind was someplace else." She sighed. "Actually, in Sicily."

She brushed her horse's chestnut coat and then his black mane. "You like that? We're going to win first place." She kissed his soft muzzle.

Maddie was fortified with a new determination to get her life back to the way it was before. Before *the Big Jilting.*

After the show, Maddie drove home from Santa Barbara.

Her condo was now finished with new everything. The wood floors had been sanded and stained a light grey. The kitchen table and bar stools were sea-foam green. The sectional in the living room was a sand color and end tables in light blue. Both the master and guest bedrooms had all new furniture. She'd gone so far as describing to her decorator the exact type of accent chair she wanted in the master bedroom.

That night, she jumped up out of a sound sleep. "Where? Oh… no, I was dreaming of Giorgio again. This time I was in his bed." She shook her head. "How do I get you out of my mind? I—"

She threw her covers off and ran to the shower. "That's what I need. An ice-cold shower." *Ice.*

She smiled and thought back to the time she'd asked Giorgio if he had ice cubes for her glass of water. He'd said, "We really don't use any, but I'll ask Maria to make some just for you." His eyes had smoldered into hers when he said that.

When they returned from Erice and Marsala, he'd brought her up to his room and after the hot bath they had shared, he played with her. Running an ice cube between her breasts, around her nipples, and down past her navel. Giorgio had to get another one before he reached her mound. Telling her to spread her legs, he'd inserted the ice cube into her vagina. *"Let's see how long before you melt that."*

Giorgio took another cube into his mouth, and his cold tongue licked her clit. He had teased her body into an amazing orgasm. She'd taken her turn too, teasing his body.

Maddie shut the water off in her lonely shower. She wrapped a towel around her body and dried her hair. It was only seven a.m. She would get to work early today before the other employees arrived. Dressed in one of her grey business suits with matching straight-leg pants and her navy stilettos, she drove to the bank. Taking the elevator to the top floor, she prayed that she didn't see anyone. Her dark-lensed sunglasses covered the darker smudges under her eyes; the concealer she'd applied hadn't helped.

I have to focus on work and forget Giorgio. A knock on her office door interrupted her thoughts. "Come in."

Traci walked in with two cups of coffee. She handed one to Maddie. "Black, no sugar, extra strong."

"Thanks, you're a lifesaver." Maddie sipped the coffee.

Traci sat in the chair facing Maddie's desk, taking the lid off her coffee cup. "We have a busy day today, and tomorrow, you have that dinner meeting with Mr. Cosimoto."

Maddie took another sip of coffee before she said, "I think you should come with me to dinner, so you can get a feel for what he wants and how Watson Financial can be of service."

"If you think he won't feel as if he were being dumped on me. He was concerned when you took over. How will he feel now?"

"I'll explain. We both know that you're the best person for his interests. He's a smart businessman and will realize that you'll be a better fit for him." Maddie smiled.

Traci visibly sighed. "I'll tell Bob that I won't be home for dinner tomorrow night."

"Your husband is supportive and knows how hard you work. I'm sure he'll understand. You were always going to be promoted. You've been amazing, helping me get up to speed after being away for so long. You deserve this."

She blushed. "Thank you. And you're right, Bob is verry supportive of me. Anyway." She clapped. "On to a fun subject. How was the show?"

Maddie smiled. "I won a blue ribbon. But really, it felt good to be in the arena again. I haven't competed in years, and I almost forgot how much I love it. I'm thinking of taking it up again."

Traci smiled. "That's great. I'm happy for you." She shifted in her seat and frowned.

"You okay?" Maddie asked.

Traci fidgeted a bit. "Doug wanted to go to Santa Barbara this weekend to see you. But Bob steered him away from going."

"Thank you for telling me and tell Bob thank you as well." She smiled. "I've made it abundantly clear to Doug though that I want nothing at all to do with him. I'll be professional in our business dealings, but other than that, I don't want to know him."

"You do know they split up? Nancy wants a divorce."

"Yes, well…" She shrugged. "That's their business."

Traci left to go back to her desk. Maddie pushed her chair back and walked around her desk to stand in front of the wall of windows. The Pacific looked so choppy today. A storm was brewing, and Maddie had the same feeling about her life. A storm raged inside her.

She visualized Giorgio, naked—a Roman statue—come to life. To… what is the word? She needed. Yes! Needs, desires, wants, all of that. She had to get away—but where to? She'd been home from Palermo a month now, and other than that brief text when she arrived home, she and Giorgio hadn't been in contact.

Glancing at her wristwatch, she did a quick calculation. They were in the middle of *riposo* right about now. *Who is he resting with?* Fighting with herself, she grabbed her phone, then quickly placed it back on the desk. She took a step back, glanced at the phone, and picked it up again.

She texted one word. Hi

Maddie closed her eyes and shook her head. *Why did I do that?* Seconds dragged like minutes, then a ping. Hi, yourself. *Smiley face.*

She frowned. There was no information in that response.

What was she going to text back? How are you? Who's in your bed? She went for it and texted. Miss me?

Always. Come to me.

She looked at the text for a moment then without thinking, she wrote, Next week.

Meet me in Rome… Maddalena.

Rome???

Yes. I have a business meeting there, but we can have… what… ever you want.

She smiled at that. He knew her so well. Lots of sex.

Will book a flight. *Wink face.*

She walked back to her desk with a silly grin on her face, staring at the blank screen of her phone. Maddie turned on her laptop and opened a recent file on her latest client. Then she sat back for a moment and composed an email to Michael and cc'd her father. We should promote Traci to my position.

She deleted the draft. *Tonight, I will talk to them. In person would be better.*

CHAPTER 7

Traffic was always horrendous in LA, so avoiding the freeways, Maddie took Wilshire Boulevard to Beverly Hills. She drove up to her parents' French provincial-style home and parked her silver BMW in the driveway next to her brother's red Mercedes. *Good. Michael's here. We can talk after dinner.*

She rang the front doorbell, and her mother opened the door. "Oh my God. What is wrong with you?"

"Hello to you too, Mom. I don't know what you mean," Maddie replied as she kissed her mother on the cheek.

"Honey, the dark circles. What is it? What's bothering you?"

"Let's go in. I see Michael is here." Maddie heard scampering as a pink cloud came running across the white-porcelain-tile entry.

"Aunt Maddie, you're here."

Madeline picked up her niece and hugged her. "Yes, sweetie. Have you been a good girl?"

The mop of blonde curls bounced, almost dropping the plastic tiara from her head. "Do you have something for me?"

"Charlotte!" her grandmother said.

Maddie ignored her mother and said, "In my purse." She stood the little girl on her feet, then crouched down, unzipped her designer bag, and took out a box wrapped in pink paper.

Charlotte took the gift and ran into the living room. "Mamma, Daddy, Aunt Maddie brought me a present."

Maddie and her mom followed from the entry, walking into the formal living room.

"Madeline, you spoil her terribly," her mother said.

"She's so spoilable," Maddie said.

They laughed, and Maddie's mother hugged her. "I hope you'll tell me what's bothering you."

"I will, Mom, but not right this minute. Why don't we have lunch tomorrow? Just you and me."

Her mother smiled. "Yes, lunch and shopping on Rodeo Drive."

Maddie smiled. "Sounds perfect."

When they reached the living room, Maddie went to her dad and kissed him on the cheek. "How are you feeling?"

"I'm much stronger and ready to get back to work."

The Watson clan in unison said, "No!"

"Dad, it's way too soon," Maddie said.

Her mother went over to her husband. She leaned her hip against the arm of his chair and hugged him. "I like having you home. It reminds me of when we were first married, before the kids."

"Really, dear?" he said.

Maddie watched a blush spread across her mother's cheeks before she said, "Well, not quite. You *are* recovering from heart surgery. Nevertheless, I like having you home."

Mr. Watson patted his wife's hand and then brought it to his lips to kiss. Maddie melted at the love between her parents. That type of love no longer existed. Or did it simply miss her? She glanced at her brother and sister-in-law. They had the same look in their eyes as her parents. Maddie turned away. She had to get out of this funk. Rome would relax her and get her back on track. Maddie fought the urge to get on a plane to Sicily this second and would wait out the week before flying to Giorgio in Rome.

THE WATSON FAMILY walked into the formal dining room. The table was set with her mother's favorite china in a pattern that matched the décor of the house. Crystal-fluted glasses for wine and water at each place setting. All, but Charlotte, who had a special dinner set with Disney princesses around the border of the plate and the matching cup.

From the dining room, French doors led to a lush green backyard and a pool. The landscaping lights were on as well as the pool lights, in a rainbow of changing colors. Maddie loved this view. She had missed her family so much.

"I understand that you and Sir Prance A Lot won first place," her mom said.

"Yes, it was good to be competing again. I think I'm going to take up competition again."

Maddie glanced around the dinner table at her family. "Will we be going to Maui for Christmas this year?"

Her father said, "Yes. I'm feeling better, getting stronger each day. Hawaii is where we have gone for the past five years. It has become our family tradition."

"I always appreciated that you did this for me, so we could spend the holidays together."

Maddie was happy to be home; the time she had lived away from her family had been difficult but needed. Now though, after the scare of her father's surgery, she didn't want to miss any more time with them. Living in LA would be good. She would make it so, although she would have to avoid Doug. He made it uncomfortable for her to be at work, but she would have to deal with that. She couldn't let him affect her that way anymore.

Maddie didn't love him, but she didn't hate him either; she had no feelings but that deep-seated anger. Anger at his betrayal with her best friend. Doug had humiliated her. Hurt her and taught Maddie never to give her heart to anyone or to trust ever again. Now, *she* used people.

Doug's words haunted her, "Nancy's a better lover than you can ever be. She gives me what I want in bed. I need that in my relationship, more than marrying you for your money and the bank." Each time Maddie thought of those words, the old familiar knot in her throat grew. She struggled, determined to find the courage she'd relied on since Doug turned his back on her and walked out of her life.

After dinner, the Watson clan retired to the family room at the back of the house. The cozy room had a thick, cream-colored carpet on the floor and two comfortable mint-green fabric couches, separated by a coffee table. The big-screen TV at the moment was playing a children's show for Charlotte, as she sat on the floor playing with the doll Maddie had given her.

Maddie asked, "Dad, can I talk with you and Michael?"

"Yes, dear. Let's go into my study."

They excused themselves and went into her father's study. Growing up, this room had definitely been one of Maddie's favorites. Two walls of the room held bookshelves filled with classics and modern books. A rolling ladder hung from the top rail to reach the uppermost books. Maddie had loved to come into the study, take a book, and sit in the corner by the window, looking out over the garden and read.

"I'm happy to have helped you on the deal with Lombardo Wines."

Her dad said, "I understand that Mr. Lombardo was very gracious and invited you to stay at his home."

This wasn't where she wanted the conversation to go. Remembering Giorgio's sensuous lips on her body, a vision of him lying in bed in all of his naked glory before he rolled her under him flooded her mind. She squirmed in her seat.

"He's a businessman and saw a good deal. Actually, a great bargain for the vineyard, all that property, equipment, and a thirty-five-room mansion. Mr. Lombardo did very well for himself. He knew even before I arrived, his cash offer would entice us to accept the lower offering price. We didn't need any other banks involved. Our loss on that property was minimal, and we closed the books on it. The economy is stabilizing after this last downturn, and we'll be in a better position with some of our other short sales. Watson Financial is a solid institution."

"So, what's on your mind?" her brother asked.

"Well, I would like to do something different, and I think we should promote Traci to my position. She has been a driving force with the portfolios I brought back from Japan and also the portfolios you've assigned me in your absence, Dad. She should have been promoted awhile ago."

"We spoke with her before you came back from Japan. She knew she would be promoted. At the time, we gave her the raise that went along with the promotion, and once she does assume your position, she'll receive another raise," said Mr. Watson.

"What is it that you want to do, Maddie?" her brother asked.

"I'm not sure, but I know it isn't in finance or loss mitigation." She turned to look at her father. "Dad, I will stay until you're better and ready to go back to the bank."

He looked at Michael and then said to Maddie, "Madeline, I plan on turning the reigns over to your brother. This scare made me realize that I want to work less and be at home more. Spend time with your mother, maybe travel. Michael is capable of taking over, and you don't have to worry. You pursue whatever course will make you happy."

Tears stung her eyes. Maddie jumped out of her seat and hugged her father. "Oh, Dad, I love you so much. You've always been supportive of me." She turned and hugged her brother. "Congratulations, Mr. Bank President. I'm thrilled for you."

"Thanks, Sis. I knew you would be. Let me add that I understand if you choose not to stay on. But please give us some time to work all of the new changes in."

"Of course. I don't plan on leaving anytime soon. It's just that I want to eventually move on, maybe a career change. I'm young; twenty-eight isn't over the hill yet." She had been so restless at work since her return from Palermo. She wasn't focused but confused… yes, confused. Not at all her usual way.

"You have your whole life ahead of you, sweetie," her dad said. "We don't plan on making the announcement until early January. We don't want to alarm any of our employees before the holidays."

THE WEEK DRAGGED on before Maddie left to meet Giorgio in Rome. The most she'd ever seen of the Eternal City was its airports. Now, she might actually get to see the Coliseum and some other sights. But the view that had her core heat would be Giorgio in bed. When she landed and took her phone off airplane mode, there was a text from him. He would be delayed so she should check into the hotel. He would be there later this afternoon.

She was disappointed, but what was there to do? Maddie checked in, unpacked, took a shower, and then went down to the lobby. She walked over to the concierge and asked, "Can you find me a taxi with a driver who speaks English? I would like to see the Colosseum."

"Certainly, Madame. Would you like a courtesy limousine to take you?"

"No, thank you. A taxi is good."

The concierge walked with her to the line of taxis in front of the hotel. Raising his hand, he pointed to the fourth taxi in line to move forward. The cab pulled to a stop in front of them, and the driver got out.

The concierge spoke in English, "Can you take Ms. Watson sightseeing? She would like to see the Coliseum and perhaps a brief tour. Charge the entry price and your fee to the hotel." Then he turned to Maddie. "Ms. Watson, will you have *pranzo* out?"

"I plan on returning by then. Would you have something waiting in my room?"

"Yes, Madame."

The driver held the back passenger door open while Maddie slid onto the seat. He walked around to the driver's side and then proceeded to turn into the traffic of Via Roma. On the way, he pointed out some sights, such as the Forum, and eventually, the Coliseum. Her driver was quite knowledgeable, and his English was perfection. After a few hours, she returned to the hotel. When the concierge saw her, he nodded, and she proceeded up in the elevator to the top floor and her room. She opened the door, and the fragrance of gardenias filled her senses, not food. She walked into the living room of the suite and then down the hall to the bedroom.

Giorgio sat in bed, his broad shoulders against the massive headboard. He rested against two crisp, white pillows, naked. She smiled and reached to pull her blouse off. She hooked her thumbs into her slacks and shimmied both the slacks and her panties, down her legs. Leaving them on the carpeted floor.

"Ahh, Maddalena, leave the bra," he murmured.

"Really," she said, pushing her breasts together and lifting an eyebrow at him.

"Yeah. Come here," he growled in his husky voice.

Maddie needed no further encouragement. She knelt one knee on the mattress. Giorgio grabbed her waist and pulled her against him, rolling her onto her back under his rock-solid body. When he lowered his lips to hers, she tasted chocolate and mint. Giorgio's mouth was all over her at once, along with his hands.

He unhooked her bra, slipping the lacy fabric from her as his hands moved up her back and down her legs. He grazed a nipple and sucked, drawing the areola of her right breast into the heat of his mouth. Her core pulsed as a zing of pleasure shot into her belly. She melted at that and reached for his swollen flesh, stroking him. She spread her legs as he kissed her abdomen.

Tilting her pelvis, she breathed, "Come into me." She moaned, "Ahh... Now."

He reached for a condom, ripping open the packet. In her eagerness for him, she helped Giorgio roll it onto his long length. His lips found her mouth again, and his hand trailed fire down her body. One finger stroked her, drawing patterns on her sensitive flesh. Giorgio ran a long finger over her slit, pressing into her. "So nice and slick for me," he said against her lips.

Maddie tipped her hips, and her body flooded with the fire of desire for this man. She slipped her tongue into his mouth, demanding he satisfy her every need. He growled and pulled her into his arms as he pressed his erection against her. His lean, muscled body pressed into her, and she wrapped her arms around him. In one move, he thrust and stretched her as he embedded himself deep into her pulsing heat.

"Giorgio… yes, so very good."

She lifted her legs to wrap around his narrow waist, pressing him to go deeper. Faster. She needed his hard length thrusting into her over and over again. To feel his power as he possessed her. He rose above her, locking his elbows. His aqua eyes burned into her as he moved his hips, his long, thick length going deeper into her. Waves of pleasure radiated into her core, consuming her.

"Come with me," she whispered.

Giorgio groaned, and then he shuddered into her.

Panting wildly, her heart racing, she reached up her hand and felt his heartbeat pounding.

She loved that he stayed in her, kissing her neck. She practically purred, and he laughed.

"You've been—where *have* you been?" he asked.

Maddie skimmed her hands over his shoulders, breathing in his sexy scent. She wondered what he was really about to say and then answered, "I arrived early this morning. When I read your message, well, I didn't want to sit around a hotel room, so I hired a taxi to see some of the sights in Rome." She kissed his chest. Her tongue licked the slightly salty skin, teasing a flat nipple.

He looked at her naked body, his hand grazing her hip. "I like this sight the best."

"Mmm," she moaned.

"Room service delivered lunch. It's on the patio. The gas heater is on, so it should be nice and cozy out there."

"It's nice right here." She looped her arms around his

powerful neck, lifting her legs to wrap around his narrow hips again.

He moved in her. Giorgio pressed a kiss to her jaw and then with his lips in her hair, he said, "I'll be right back. Don't move." He went into the en suite and then came out, bringing another condom with him. She opened her arms, and Giorgio took her into his strong embrace.

Some time passed before Maddie walked over to the standing wardrobe and reached in for the two hotel robes. She tossed one to Giorgio and slipped the other on. They walked through the living room out to the patio where lunch was waiting. Rome spread out like a tapestry before her. Domed buildings sat in the distance, the blue sky above. She walked over to the sideboard and lifted the lids on a variety of chafing dishes. "Pasta, salad, steamed vegetables, shrimp, and lobster." She turned to Giorgio.

"No hamburgers?" she teased.

He laughed and said, "If that's what you would like, I'm sure I can find someplace in Rome that serves them. Fries too."

They filled their plates with the delicious food. Giorgio poured wine into two goblets and brought them over to the burgundy-linen-covered table. Pink-linen napkins in the shape of a fan laid at each place setting. She sipped her wine.

"Where did you go sightseeing this morning?" Giorgio asked

"I asked the taxi driver to take me to the Coliseum. This is my first time in Rome, so I wasn't sure where to go, and that's the most famous place here. I would love to see the Vatican while I'm here too."

"Yes, we can do that. And there is the Trevi Fountain. You'll have to toss a coin in, so that you'll return to Rome." He winked.

"Oh. Is that the legend?"

"It is. More wine?" He lifted the bottle, and as she nodded, he poured the flavorful white wine into her glass.

They finished their meal. Maddie fought to cover a yawn. Giorgio hugged her to him and said, "Go inside and take a nap."

He kissed her brow, and when she turned, he swatted her behind. She laughed and went into their bedroom to lie on the bed, dragging the satin comforter over her.

MADDIE'S EYES gradually opened and looked around the hotel suite's bedroom. She felt rudderless. Only in bed with Giorgio did she feel… What? Safe, cared for… Loved. Loved, there is a word—she knew he didn't love her, and she didn't love him. It was just sex and lust for them, *right?* "The best sex," he'd said, and then he had teased her about how she'd improved. The old nagging feelings of inadequacy clenched at her insides. No, he didn't know about the lies and deceit Doug had spewed at her.

Giorgio had held her, kissing her, and laughed with her, not at her. He had teased and graded her as if she were in school, and he was the professor. His skill was… *Stop this!*

Maddie walked out onto their private terrace off the bedroom. It wasn't as large as the one off the living room, where they had earlier eaten lunch. This one was large enough to hold two chaise lounges and a small table between. It was cozy and intimate.

The view of the Spanish Steps was breathtaking, but the best view of all sat on a grey chaise lounge. Giorgio's robe was parted to reveal his sculpted chest and a smattering of dark hair. His abs were sculpted perfection. She followed the line of black hair that disappeared into his cobalt-silk boxers. Her breath caught as the fabric moved with his growing arousal. She looked up as a smile lifted the corners of her mouth. His aqua stare caught her, and heat rose into her cheeks.

"Come here, Maddalena."

His eyes burned into her. She couldn't look away. Her bare feet moved on the terracotta tiles, Maddie thought, *he's a drug. I can't stop. I need him.* She reached the edge of the chaise and sat at his side. Moving forward, her hair tented around them, and her parted lips found his. He took over, kissing her thoroughly. Her nipples rubbed against her robe, aching for his touch.

This is why I came here. For this man and the power he has over my body. He held her to him, slipping his hand into her robe. Reaching a breast, he took the nipple between his thumb and forefinger, rotating, coaxing it to pebble hardness. She moaned. Giorgio played with her tongue while his fingers played with her nipple. She moved in his arms, and he lifted her to sit on his lap. His mouth never left hers, as she leaned against his massive chest, running her hands along his muscle-covered olive skin.

Maddie panted into his mouth while he slid the fire of his hand down over her abdomen. Her head fell back, and his lips scorched her neck on a path to her other breast. He covered the nipple with his mouth and held it between his teeth as the tip of his tongue licked and pressed the hard peak. Her legs fell open to his questing fingers.

Heat burned in her center as his hand glided up one inner thigh. She held her breath waiting. His long finger slid along her seam and slipped into her. She fought to hold back a moan. He sucked her nipple into his mouth and slid his finger deeper into her body. She did moan then, as she held his head to her breast and opened her legs. He slid his finger up. His thumb moved on her clitoris, applying delicious pressure. She throbbed, and her thighs trembled, as she wiggled on his lap, and his massive erection pressed into her hip.

"Yes. Oh, Giorgio." The robe was stifling, as heat radiated from her. He held her in that position.

"Please," she panted.

He lifted his gorgeous head from her breast. "Si? Yes?" His aqua gaze held a spark, and one dark brow rose.

She almost groaned. The pad of Giorgio's callused thumb slid back and forth across her sensitive clitoris.

"Ahh, oh," she did groan then.

"You have no restraint," he teased.

"No, I don't… Make me come," she whispered.

"Lie on the tile," he rasped in his Italian accent.

Maddie scrambled to the floor. Her robe opened, exposing her body to his view. He smiled down at her, taking his cobalt-silk boxers off. He left his robe on and reached into the pocket to remove a foil packet.

"Oh, no fair, you planned this." She pretended a pout.

"Are you surprised, *strega*? I am always prepared for you."

Maddie sat up, needing to touch his steel-hard shaft as he rolled the condom on. His mouth found hers again, and he laid her back onto the warm floor. Giorgio held her hips, and her hand reached down between them to guide him to her entrance. He slipped the engorged head of his erection into her, and she arched, lifting her hips for him to slide in.

"Ahhh." Maddie sighed, breathing in his masculine scent, feeling his muscular body over her, around her.

Giorgio stroked in and out deep thrusts that she eagerly met. He pistoned in and pulled almost entirely out of her, to plunge into her again and again, filling her, stretching her. Heat uncurled in her abdomen. She tried to prolong the pleasure before climaxing into an overwhelming bliss of sensations. Giorgio pumped harder and faster, giving her no time to recover before he sent her spiraling toward another powerful orgasm. By her third time, his hoarse whisper reached her through the haze of her pleasure.

"I can't hold back any longer."

She inhaled his sexy scent. "Don't," she moaned, locking her ankles around him.

Giorgio groaned and shuddered into her. Maddie held him to her breast. He brushed his lips on her neck before she rolled to her side. She looked up at a cloudless blue sky. The gas heater with their flickering flames kept the terrace warm. But it was Giorgio who warmed her blood.

They spent more time exploring each other than they did Rome. They talked while lounging in bed. He told her about his plans for the Napa vineyard and the mansion. How he wanted to convert the mansion into an intimate hotel and perhaps a wedding venue.

All too soon, Maddie boarded the commercial flight back home. He wanted to see her before Christmas, but they would have to schedule the time. It was tough though. Giorgio and his family would be in Manhattan for shopping and the theater in early December.

Maddie needed to be with her family for Christmas. After the scare from her father's heart surgery, she didn't want to miss a Christmas with her family. They always spent the holiday in Maui, and that was where she would be.

Giorgio had said that he would find the time to meet once more in November and before he flew back to Sicily in early December. Then in early January, he needed to go to France for a meeting with his vintner, about the Nice vineyard. In late January, there was a DiMarco Enterprises board meeting in NYC that he'd have to go to, so they planned for a long-distance 'let's meet for sex' relationship. She was content with that. *Yes, it's better this way. No commitments, just love—What? L U S T. Just lust and sex.*

CHAPTER 8

It was three weeks before Christmas, and Giorgio hadn't seen Maddie since the Bahamas just before Thanksgiving. After Rome, he'd texted her a photo of a villa in the Bahamas, asking her if she'd like to spend four days there where they could play on the sand and have lots of privacy. It seemed as if it were ages ago. He missed her terribly, and although Lombardo Wines and the board of DiMarco Enterprises kept him extremely busy, he felt her absence. A smile played around the corners of his mouth. He missed her sass… her spunk but what he missed the most—the way her moss-green eyes would fill with desire when she looked at his naked body.

He was in his cousin Ricardo DiMarco's penthouse apartment on the Upper East Side of Manhattan. Glancing out the window, he watched thick snowflakes fill the sky, falling to the ground twelve stories below. Giorgio slipped his phone from his pants pocket and texted Maddie.

Hi. A blizzard is predicted for NYC, and I want to get out before the airports are closed. I'm heading to the Napa vineyard a few days earlier than planned. That may give us a little more time together before I go home. Can you meet me?

He always sweated, waiting for her reply. He loved her, but he wouldn't tell her. He knew she would run away from that. He had to go slow and see if he could convince her that only her loser ex-fiancé was untrustworthy.

Now he had to find a way to convince this beautifully independent woman to be with him exclusively—another thing he wouldn't demand—just nudge her along. He wouldn't think of any other men she may be seeing. He worked at consuming all of her time. Between her working and now flying to meet him for long weekends.

Her reply came through, and he looked down at his phone

Yes. I would love to. I just don't have much time. Tying up loose ends before I go to Maui.

He smiled at that and texted back. You can tie me up.

She sent him a smiling emoji, then a quick follow-up text that he read. With a smile that tugged at his lips, he texted back. I'm getting hard just thinking about that.

GIORGIO and his cousin Lorenzo DiMarco missed the blizzard that stranded a large number of his family in NYC. They would all meet back in Sicily for Christmas.

Lorenzo was a cruise ship captain for the Contessa Cruise Lines, a DiMarco Enterprises company. Right now, Lorenzo was stationed out of San Diego. He was a free spirit, flittering from woman to woman. Happy for the no-commitment relationships he pursued, Lorenzo had visited with the family in NYC because he wouldn't make it back home in time for Christmas.

JFK International Airport was behind them as the plane

reached cruising altitude. The sun was bright as they flew above the storm clouds on their way to San Diego.

"You look hungover," Giorgio said. "Want something for your headache?"

"Yes, please."

Giorgio rang for Rosa, one of the flight attendants. He spoke in Italian, "Can you get my cousin some aspirin and mineral water?"

When she left, Lorenzo turned to Giorgio. "Thanks for the ride. Had you not offered to take me to San Diego, I would have been trapped in NY, I just know it."

"We're lucky. We were one of the last planes to be cleared before the airports closed. I didn't think it would have been too much of a hardship for you to be delayed. You seem to be doing well for yourself," Giorgio said.

"Haha. You did abandon me last night with those two beautiful women." Lorenzo put his fingers to his lips and kissed the air in a very Italian gesture.

Giorgio chuckled. "Oh, is that what you say about me having to leave you so I could see my mother. I wanted to tell her of my plans for the new vineyard I bought in Napa."

He didn't mention that although the two women were gorgeous, neither of them attracted him. Not since he met Madeline Watson. Before Maddie, his attitude had been so different. One woman was the same as another in the shadows of the night. They were all the same, and he would have happily gone with one of them or both those women and spent the night in bed with them.

Lorenzo toed off his loafers, then reclined on the couch, closing his eyes. "When you excused yourself after dinner… it was clear you didn't want to come out with us. Cecilia, the taller of the two women. Remember?"

"Yes, they were both gorgeous and interested in us."

Lorenzo turned, opened his eyes, and said, "Remember

South Beach? She suggested that I go back to their hotel room—"

Giorgio burst out laughing. "You haven't changed. Not one damn bit."

"Shh, my head is killing me." He laughed. "What beauties they were. And so inventive. You missed a really good time."

"I'll bet I did. Rest. I'll wake you before we land." Giorgio picked up his briefcase from beside his plush-leather reclining chair. "I have reports to go over. Are you sure you don't want to use one of the bedrooms? We have at least five hours before we arrive in San Diego."

"No. I just want to take a nap."

Giorgio took a sip of his mineral water and leafed through one of the latest soil reports from his vineyards in the Provence region outside of Nice. He turned on his laptop and checked the file. He searched for the benchmark report on the vine performance. His brows drew together in a frown as he scrolled to a graph of the crop yield from the previous years.

Not wanting to disturb Lorenzo, Giorgio walked to the front of the plane and went into his office. He called his personal assistant in Palermo. "Grace, I'm going over the report you forwarded to me this morning on the *Bellet* vineyard. It's quite alarming. Has Pierre contacted us? Have I missed a call from him?"

He listened to Grace as she shuffled through papers. "No," she replied.

Giorgio placed his thumb and forefinger between his brows. "The director should have been on top of this. Why hasn't Pierre called? Something isn't right. I'll need you to set up another soil sample before my meeting with him. Be sure to ask them to double check the nitrogen levels in the soil. Tell the lab to put a rush on it. I'm on my way to Napa Valley.

Let me know when you hear from the new distributor I hired for the North American region."

After he finished his call to his PA, he called his architect to see if he could move their meeting up. He wanted to meet at the property so that his overseer would be there as well.

When Giorgio arrived at the vineyard, the architect had already drawn up preliminary plans for the standalone building that would become a restaurant he wanted to have at the winery. She was efficient. He liked the way she'd incorporated the sleek lines of modern design and the ambiance of traditional old world. Many of the vineyards had tasting rooms that were open to the public. It was an idea that had always interested him, to have more than just a tasting room, but an upscale restaurant serving the finest food pared with great wine.

He turned his attention to the mansion. It was big, and with some modifications, could become an intimate hotel. Giorgio planned to persuade his mother to take charge of that project and eventually run the hotel. It would give her something to do, and he hoped she would be happy working on that.

It was cabernet season now, and he sat on one of the chaise lounges scattered around the brick and stone patio at the back of the house. The fire pit had been lit, and he enjoyed a glass of red wine. It had rained earlier; the air smelled clean and fresh. Arcing across the late-afternoon sky was a rainbow. He watched it for a while, sipping his wine. He was happy with the progress he'd made today.

His thoughts turned to Madeline. One more delay, and he would tell Maddie to stay in LA; he could just as easily fly down to her. She was so stubborn not wanting to use his jet. Refusing to allow him to buy her anything. He texted her. Why don't I fly down to you? I can be there in a few hours.

His phone pinged. Oh, could you? That would be great. I

have to finish this report by tonight. Can you get a Lyft from the airport?

He chuckled at that. Thinking he had another Lamborghini in the cargo hold of his private jet.

He texted back. You do know I have my own plane and transportation?

His phone lit up. My bad. Hehe. She texted back.

He sent a smiley face back, then called his pilot. The flight crew knew there were times when he needed to travel at a moment's notice, and they were always prepared for him. He promised them that they would all be back with their families in Palermo for Christmas.

MADDIE CHECKED HER PHONE. Giorgio had texted that he was out front. She smiled at the knock on the door and checked the peephole before opening it. Since the incident with Doug, she'd become cautious before opening her door.

Maddie had dressed or *undressed* only for Giorgio. Red stiletto heels and a black thong were all she wore. She ran her fingers through her hair, pulling the long, blonde tresses to one side. She'd left her hair loose to curl down her shoulder and over her breast. Opening the door, she stepped away for Giorgio to enter.

"Oh, you dressed for me," he said as he dropped his overnight bag on the entry floor. He slipped his arm around her neck, dragging her against his expansive chest, and brushed her lips with gentle, sweeping motions.

Maddie slid her hands up his arms, feeling the toned muscles of his biceps, and onto his broad-sculpted shoulders. Her hands drifted to the nape of his neck. Her fingers plunged into his thick, dark hair. She sparred with his tongue, missing how good he made her feel.

She lifted one leg, rubbing it up his flank. A surge of hot desire shot into her center. Giorgio held her to him, sliding his palm over her hip, dragging her closer. Then he cupped her buttocks, lifting her to wrap her legs around his waist.

Giorgio kissed her jaw. "Where is your bedroom?" he growled against her neck before nipping her skin.

She wrapped her legs around his waist. "To the left is the master bedroom. I already turned the covers down."

Locking her ankles, she wiggled in his arms and unbuttoned his shirt. She held him closer as he thoroughly kissed her, sucking her bottom lip into his mouth, running his tongue along her teeth.

She pressed against his muscle-clad chest, his hair exciting her nipples. "Hurry," she panted into his mouth.

He laid her on the cool sheets of her new bed, and he ripped at his clothes. Unzipping his fly and dropping his slacks to the floor. She knelt on the bed, touching his erection, feeling her power as he got harder in her hand. Maddie smiled up at him before she lowered herself to kiss the velvety tip of his erection, sliding her tongue over the swollen head, and eagerly taking him into her mouth.

He brushed her hair to the side, cupping her head for a heartbeat. "It is too much. I… want ahh… ahh, no. I want to be in you." His Italian accent thickened.

Maddie relented at the sound of his plea because she really did want him to come in her.

"*Strega*, let me get a condom."

Her fingers brushed his shoulders. "I have a surprise for you."

He raised one dark brow, and a devilish glint held her. "More than the greeting at your door?"

Her voice was shakier than she would have liked as she said, "I started the pill and now am safely on it long enough for you not to need one… if you want."

"Oh, I want," he growled. "I want to feel you around me. My bare skin surrounded by your wet heat is my greatest desire."

He bent, and she reached up to his lips, losing herself in Giorgio's kiss, his lips, his tongue. His fingers stroked over her belly, dragging fire over her skin. She opened herself to him. When one of Giorgio's long fingers entered her, she whispered, "I'm ready."

"Yes, I feel how ready you are," he groaned against her lips, swirling his finger in her.

Later, there would be time for her to use her mouth after the rush of lust and desire was sated, then they could go at their leisure. But now, only hard and fast would satisfy her.

They spent the remainder of the night in bed. She lay on her side with Giorgio against her back, his knees tucked under hers. He twined their fingers together and in his low husky voice, he sang an Italian song. In between the words, he kissed her neck, behind her ear, nibbling on her sensitive skin. At one point, she wiggled against his erection, and he dragged her under his body, throwing her legs over his shoulders and in one thrust, he buried himself to the hilt. She missed the way he stretched her and filled her.

In a tremulous whisper, she said, "I want you to stay in me all night."

"Remember *Erice?*" He gave her a blazing look. "You didn't sleep all night."

"Yes… just like that."

Maddie did doze and then woke up to the light caress of Giorgio's hand over her buttock. She stretched, arching her back, and smothered a yawn. *It's not a dream; he's here in my bed!*

"Get up, lazy head. Let's go for a sunrise swim," he said, leaning into her.

She gazed into his aqua eyes, a smile spreading across her lips as she rubbed her leg along his thigh.

"No, no, *Maddalena*. First swimming, then breakfast, and a shower."

"Oh, you. Okay, we'll go swimming first, but for me, the water is too cold. I have to put on my wet suit."

"I will keep you warm." He tugged her to him and kissed her lips.

"I have to warn you, the beach here is public. It isn't like when we stayed at that villa in the Bahamas. Here anyone can be walking by." She held back a moan as he sucked one of her nipples into his mouth, his tongue licking the pointed peak the same way he licked her clit.

"So, I have to wear my bathing trunks? Is that what you are implying?" His beard tickled her breasts as he spoke.

"Well… it may… be… a… good idea… I wouldn't want to fight anyone for you. Let's stay in bed. Keep doing what you're doing."

He sat up, and Maddie laughed. Giorgio grabbed her waist and swung her from the bed. "Okay, go and put on your wet suit if you must. I packed my trunks."

She stopped and turned to watch him in all his naked glory, as he bent over his suitcase. The sculpted muscles of his back rippled with his movements, reminding her how they felt under her fingers when he pumped his long, hard cock into her.

"I hope you brought something big enough to cover all of your equipment."

He laughed, "Believe me, I want only you to see and use my *equipment*. Come on, let's hurry."

She slipped into her fuchsia and blue full-body wet suit while they were joking. Barefoot with her hair loose, she twirled in front of Giorgio. "This definitely isn't the string bikini I wore in the Bahamas." She laughed.

"Wow, you weren't kidding."

"I wear this when I go surfing."

He took her hand, and they walked out of the bedroom. They hurried down the wooden steps of her house and onto the sandy beach, then they ran into the early morning surf. The water was cold, but Giorgio didn't seem to mind. He held her to him for a moment, and she watched a devilish smile take over his handsome face before he lifted her into the air and dropped her into the water. She came up sputtering, her hair flying in all directions, spraying him with droplets of saltwater.

"Oh, you wait until I get you for that, *strega*."

They ran and chased each other in the surf, playing and laughing. She saw an opportunity to tackle him, sending Giorgio to the ground with her on top of him.

"Oh no, please don't hurt me," he teased.

"You! You let me catch you, now didn't you?" She rolled over to lie on the wet sand.

Giorgio rolled on top of her, pushing her hair from her face. He smiled at her, capturing her gaze. "You caught me... back in Sicily."

"I—"

He bent and kissed her lips. She forgot what she was going to say as he kissed her. A long, leisurely kiss that warmed her.

He stood. Taking her hands, he yanked her to her feet. "I think we should take that shower before breakfast."

They ran up the wooden steps that led to the entry off the terrace and through the living room to Maddie's bedroom. Giorgio turned on the shower while Maddie collected shampoo and towels from the linen closet. They both stepped into the hot, steamy shower. Maddie took the bar of soap and rubbed it between her hands, making a frothy lather of bubbles, then she ran her soapy hands over his broad-muscled chest.

Giorgio squeezed some shampoo into the palm of his hand and lathered her hair. They laughed and joked while washing the sand and saltwater from their bodies. Maddie stroked her hand over Giorgio's abdomen, inching lower.

He tugged her to him. Wrapping his arms around her waist, he said, "Later, *strega*. Right now, I'm starving for real food."

"No time for a quickie?" She pretended to pout, but she was hungry too. "I guess I'll have to feed you. We didn't really eat… food, that is, last night."

"We'll do that and more again later. Right now, I have an important question. Can you cook? Or do we have to go out?"

She was so blissfully happy. "I think I can manage eggs and toast, maybe a cheese omelet."

He turned off the shower, and they dried each other. Her hands lingered on him, and she watched as Giorgio's flesh came alive. He hugged her to him and then swatted her buttock.

"After breakfast, I promise not to let you out of bed until we go to dinner." Giorgio smiled. "I made reservations for eight o'clock."

Fear gripped at Maddie's chest. "Where?" She tried for casual. "Do we have to… I mean… what type of cuisine?"

She hoped he didn't hear the concern in her voice. How would he know where she and Doug had gone when they were dating and during their engagement? After all, there were hundreds and hundreds of restaurants in LA.

Giorgio said, "Luna's on the ocean. They have fire pits."

The most romantic restaurant in Malibu—where Doug had proposed.

"Madeline. Would you rather stay in?"

"No. I would love to go out with you and enjoy a nice dinner."

She picked up his t-shirt and slipped it over her head and down her body. Giorgio stepped into his jeans, and then Maddie watched him take his cordless shaver from his case. She stood next to him at the master bathroom sink while he shaved, and she dried her hair. *Don't think. Just enjoy this intimate time.*

Over the low buzz of his shaver, he said, "Then we can go to a nightclub if you don't mind driving." He put his shaver down and took a bottle of his aftershave out, splashing some on. "You did suggest I take a Lyft. I can order a limo, then we won't have to worry about driving."

Maddie breathed his wonderful spicy scent. "I'll drive. You know I don't drink too much." She took the bottle and put her finger over the opening, turning the aftershave so that some wet her finger. Then she rubbed it onto her neck.

While Maddie made an omelet, Giorgio cut up some fruit he found in the fridge and put up a pot of coffee. "I'm going to have to teach you how to make espresso."

"I miss that nice, dark brew, but I'm going to have to get a special pot. I looked for those wonderful pastries... what were they called... little horns."

"*Cornetto*." He smiled. "I remember you *especially* loved the ones with the chocolate hazelnut filling. Perhaps we can find some."

"How long can you stay?" Maddie asked, as they sat in the breakfast nook.

"Just a few days. I have to get home for meetings in Palermo."

Maddie loaded the dishes into the dishwasher. "I usually don't cook enough to use my dishwasher, so this is a treat to play homemaker."

He slipped his arms around her waist, and she leaned

back against him. Giorgio nipped her neck then said, "Let's go play in bed." Turning her, he lifted her over his shoulder fireman style.

She laughed. "Oh no, put me down."

He slowed his steps. "Are you sure?"

She slid one hand into the waistband of his jeans and down to a butt cheek. She squeezed and rubbed his granite-hard butt. "Well… may… be." Her hand slid around to his erection. "Oh yes, put me down on this."

He tossed her onto the bed and had his jeans off before she bounced up. He lay on his back. Maddie giggled, kneeling on the mattress, and with a provocative pose, her knees spread as she gripped the hem of his t-shirt, pulling it over her head and completely off her body.

She leaned over and straddled his waist. "So big and hard," she said, holding his erect cock and marveling at how her fingers didn't meet around him. He reached up to her breasts, his thumb and forefinger plucking her nipples.

"Oh, I want… Giorgio…"

He leaned up, pulling her to him as his lips pressed hers. Against her mouth, he whispered, "Take me and put me where you want me."

Maddie held back a moan as she rose up enough to hold his engorged erection at the entrance to her hot core. She eased herself down, taking his hard length inch by inch into her. He kissed her as she seated herself fully on him. She never got tired of feeling him so big and so hard in her. Giorgio held her lips with his in a kiss that grew deeper with each sweep of his tongue. His long fingers spread on her waist, keeping her down on him.

Slowly, she rocked forward and then back. Moaning, she broke the kiss. A smile lifted the corners of her lips, the lids of her eyes slowly closed, and her head fell back at the bliss-fully hot sensations he brought her.

"You look so pleased with yourself—"

"And you feel so good." She squeezed her inner muscles.

"Ahh, there is my *strega*."

Maddie opened her eyes and looked into the aqua fire of Giorgio's gaze. "I want—"

"What do you want?"

"More screwing and less talking," she said as she lifted and lowered herself on his length, enjoying the friction of him pumping up into her as she pushed down on him.

They spent the day as he'd said, in bed. Maddie yearned for this feeling, so nice to lie in his strong arms.

They watched the sunset from her bed, then Giorgio went to get ready for their evening out. He wore a three-piece, custom-made suit, with a silk shirt and a tie that brought out the aqua of his eyes. His cufflinks she guessed were white gold and, on his wrist, a solid-gold wristwatch. Maddie chose a red sequin bandage mini dress with a scoop neck. She put on her very pricy stiletto sandals with the straps decorated with crystal cherry blossoms that wrapped around her ankles, stopping below her calf.

Luna's was further north on the Pacific Coast Highway in a secluded area of beach in Malibu. The indoor restaurant opened onto the sand where dining tables were set up almost to the water's edge. They were led to a table closer to the interior. Giorgio asked, "Is this acceptable, Maddalena?"

"Oh yes, thank you."

Giorgio nodded his approval to the host, and then Giorgio pulled out Maddie's chair for her to sit. The host moved to the opposite chair and held it out. Giorgio said, "Let's have champagne to begin."

"Very well, sir." He turned to go.

Giorgio reached across the table and held her hand. "Have I told you how beautiful you are, the most desirable woman I have ever met?"

She felt her cheeks heat at his words. She gently squeezed his hand. "I'm very happy that you were able to get here before you go home."

They had steak and lobster, and she chose a slice of carrot cake for dessert. When their waiter brought out the dessert, strategically placed on her plate, along with the cake, sat a cornetto. She looked up at Giorgio, he said, "They aren't just for breakfast. I made sure to get you the one with the hazelnut filling."

After the fabulous dinner, they walked along a path near the beach before going to the nightclub he had told her about. He ordered sparkling water at the club, and they danced through the night. It was close to five in the morning when she pulled her car into the garage. They climbed the interior steps hand in hand. In the entry, she leaned her head against his chest. In a mellow voice, she said, "I had a great time."

He kissed her temple. "Did I make new memories for you?"

She lifted her head, looking into his eyes. "Yes, you've given me the best memories. Thank you."

She realized that he knew of her concern, but he did make her forget her past. He held her, and they walked into the bedroom.

"I can stay a few more days, and then I have to go back to Palermo. When do you go to Maui?"

"Next week. What about you?"

Giorgio snuggled her against him, kissing her cheek. "We will be all together at my uncle's villa, both Christmas Eve and Christmas Day. You remember my housekeeper Maria? Her family will be flying in from Milan, and she will use my villa to entertain them."

"That's so nice of you to let her family stay like that."

He shrugged. "She doesn't like to fly, and her family had better job opportunities in the north."

"What about your mother?" Maddie asked, cautiously.

"She will be there, probably causing trouble and nagging me. Telling me that I have wasted my education."

"I've read the prospectus on DiMarco Enterprises *and* one of their subsidiaries—Lombardo Wines. It's not too shabby. I can't imagine why she's complaining."

"I'm not the CEO."

"What? That's her complaint? You're happy at what you do… I… read what your profits were… *and*… your income!"

"What else did you read?" His husky Italian accent sent shivers of delight up her spine.

She smiled, reaching for his tie, slipping it through his shirt collar. "That… the president is single, thirty-four… and—"

He kissed her. "Yes, go on. What else?"

"The… best lay I've ever had." She unbuttoned his vest, pushing his jacket and then his vest off his shoulders and down his arms.

He looked at her with a shocked expression. "That was in the prospectus?"

"No. But it's the truth. Now, come sex with me. We don't have much time before you leave, and I won't see you again until after the New Year."

"Come to my cousin Gianni's wedding."

She shook her head. "I *don't* do weddings."

He lifted her in his arms. "That chair reminds me of the one in *Erice*, remember?"

"Oh, yes. I remember *everything*," she said in a hoarse whisper.

"Then sit in it for me." He reached to pull her dress over her head and groaned, "No bra *and* no panties. What kind of a club did you think we were going to?" He dropped her dress to the floor. "Is this how you SoCal girls go clubbing? I'm glad I didn't know about this sooner."

She couldn't help the throaty laugh that escaped her as she sat. Slowly, she lifted one leg over the arm of the chair and then the other. He knelt, and she watched as he looked at her. Knowing she was fully exposed to him, she held her breath.

"So wet already," he said, leaning forward.

"Yes, for you," she whispered.

He kissed her mouth with gentle sweeps of his lips. Maddie held his cheeks and thrust her tongue into his mouth, sliding her tongue over his. Giorgio moved his hand down to her breast, and his other arm around her waist, as he increased the pressure of his kiss. Maddie guided Giorgio's hand down her abdomen to her spread legs.

"You have no patience," he murmured against her lips.

"I know. I need you."

"Okay. I won't make you wait." He trailed kisses down her stomach as he spoke against her skin.

Giorgio's hot breath added to her excitement. His fingers spread her, and she lifted her hips for the slide of his tongue into her core. Maddie reached to caress his head, and her fingers tangled in his thick, dark hair. Giorgio's tongue was magic, knowing just what she needed. She lost herself as his tongue explored and lashed inside her.

She arched into him. "Giorgio, oh, yes." She writhed against his mouth on the brink of a powerful orgasm. "So hot and wild."

His tongue circled her clit and then thrust into her.

Pleasure rocketed through Maddie, sending her soaring. Giorgio drove his tongue into her over and over as she climaxed in waves of mindless ecstasy. She sat panting, and he lifted her in his arms and brought her to the bed. She lay against the pillows, her breathing returning to normal while Giorgio took off his cufflinks and wristwatch.

Maddie knelt on the bed as he unbuttoned his shirt. She unzipped his pants. She was overwhelmed by the desire to give him the same pleasure he'd given her. "It's your turn to let me do whatever I want."

"You won't have any argument from me. I'm all yours to do with as you wish." He throbbed in her hand as he spoke.

Maddie looked into his aqua eyes and said, "Then lie down."

He did, and Maddie loved the thrill of making Giorgio lose control. His shout filled the bedroom as he filled her mouth. The sounds of his pleasure filled her with a feeling she'd never experienced before. He dragged her on top of him, and they fell asleep as the sun rose.

THAT AFTERNOON, Giorgio sat on her living room couch, barefoot and shirtless, wearing light-blue chino shorts, with the waistband unbuttoned and the fly half down. He rested his ankle over his thigh and held his phone in his big hand. His long, tanned fingers flew across the screen, going through his emails. Maddie had put on his t-shirt, loving how his scent clung to the fabric and surrounded her. She'd tied her hair away from her face, allowing the long, blonde tail to tumble down her back. She padded to the kitchen to make a pot of coffee for both of them. They'd slept late and now were lounging around. There was a loud and persistent banging on her front door. A male voice shouted, "Mad, Mad."

"Ugg, oh no," she groaned.

Giorgio stood. His dark brows came together. "What the hell? Who is that?"

Maddie shook her head. "It's my ex. I told him to leave me alone. He texted earlier and also left me a voicemail." The banging continued. "I sent my assistant a text to see if there's anything so urgent I would need to talk to him… There isn't."

Giorgio's lips had thinned, and his jaw set in stone. He nodded and said, "I'll take care of this."

Maddie rested her hand on his arm. "We'll *both* take care of it."

"*Si*, Maddalena. You open the door."

Maddie did, and Giorgio stepped next to her, placing his arm around her waist. Doug looked thunderstruck. "Who is this guy, Mad?"

Giorgio turned her toward him, and Maddie laid her open palm on his bare chest, resting her cheek against his shoulder. "I'm the guy who is sharing her bed now. You had better go, and don't let me find out you are bothering Madeline. I won't put up with you stalking her."

Maddie looked at Doug before adding, "I told you I would call security. I'm going to file an incident report. Now. Go." Maddie stepped back into Giorgio's body and slammed her front door closed. She turned the lock.

Giorgio pulled her into him again and held her. She wrapped her arms around his waist and rested her cheek against his chest. "I'm sorry you had to be here for that scene," she said.

"Has he bothered you often?" Giorgio's voice was hard, but then he kissed the crown of her head.

"When I got back from Sicily, he had come to my office to let me know he and Nancy, the one he jilted me for, are getting a divorce, and he wanted to get back together with me."

Giorgio stiffened. Maddie held him to her, running her fingers over his muscular back. "I told him then that I wasn't interested, and to leave me alone." She left out the time she found him lying in her bed.

"I can have around-the-clock security here in ten minutes. Let me make a call." He took out his phone.

"Giorgio." She placed a hand on his chest. "I can take care of this myself. If you weren't here, I wouldn't have opened the door, and I would have called the security company that patrols this area." She hugged him then gazed up into his aqua eyes. "I'm grateful you were here. Maybe now he will realize that I've moved on. I hope it will sink into his thick skull."

"Maddalena—"

She reached her fingers to his lips. "No. Please… Kiss me."

He growled and took her lips in an all-consuming kiss. Standing on tiptoe, she fitted herself to Giorgio's hard body. It was ecstasy when he slanted his mouth over hers. Her knees weakened, and he lifted her in his arms. Maddie wrapped her legs around his waist, her arms pulling him to her as she dug her fingers into the thick hair at his nape. She ached for more.

He returned to the couch, and she straddled him. His hands skimmed along her buttocks, pulling up his t-shirt, stroking her breasts, sparking nerve endings that ignited in her core.

She pulled at his waistband and drew the zipper the rest of the way down his shorts. Giorgio hooked his thumbs into the band while lifting his hips as Maddie shifted herself and helped to pull his shorts down his thighs. He reached under the t-shirt she wore, dragging it off her.

She loosened her hair, shaking her head, and the tresses curled around them. His hands skimmed along her naked body down over her ribs and on to her abdomen, setting off a chain reaction. Her core heated with her juices in anticipation of his fingers. Only his touch could put out the fires he'd started.

The mewling sounds finally penetrated her brain. It was her whimpering for Giorgio. He touched her clitoris with a gentle pressure. She pushed herself forward, wanting more, then she lifted herself to hold his massive erection at her opening. His eyes turned a deep aqua blue. She pushed down on him.

"Ahh… *vita mia. Si.*" His gaze raked her.

Maddie's breath hitched. "Oh, Giorgio. Please… more."

He bit her nipple and pressed one finger on her clit. With his other arm around her waist, he dragged her down the length of his cock. "Maddie."

She clung to him. His lips at her ear, he nipped her lobe, sending shivers down her spine. "Please, Giorgio, make me come."

"You feel so good and tight surrounding me with your wet heat." His words rasped.

She lifted and lowered herself on him. He pressed her clit, and she felt the first tremor of her orgasm. "Oh, yes. Yes. Yes." Shudder after shudder, she melted into him. He pushed her hair from her face, kissing her.

"Hold on, *strega.*"

He moved from the couch and laid her on the plush area rug. Taking a throw pillow from the couch, he put it under her hips. Then he buried himself in her. Thrusting deeply, he pulled almost fully out and went deeper, grinding against her. She loved when he did that, and she begged him for more.

She screamed, and Giorgio thrust a half-dozen more times before he shouted, and his hot spurts of cum filled her. He wrapped his arms around her head, driving himself to the hilt. She bit the side of his neck, tasting his salty skin as her breath returned to normal.

In the glow of their passion, he said, "Where is that coffee you were making?"

She giggled against his chest. "Yes, coffee sounds good right about now. Let me get it."

"No, you stay right where you are. I'll get the coffee. Why don't we stay in tonight?" he suggested.

"Order from the Japanese restaurant down the road and maybe watch a movie?" she asked.

"I can't remember the last time I did anything like that. We can snuggle on the couch," he said.

"Yes, that sounds nice and so relaxing. Other than the occasional Disney princess movie I've watched with my niece, I can't remember just staying in."

MADDIE WISHED Giorgio could stay longer, but all too soon, she drove him to the Santa Monica Airport where his jet was ready and waiting. She pulled her car into a parking space near the terminal entrance.

"Don't get out. I may throw you over my shoulder and carry you on to my plane."

"Ha, ha, we both have work and family to be with."

He leaned over and kissed her. Then he opened the door and got out of her car. She pressed the trunk release so he could get his overnight case. He closed the trunk and came around to the driver's side of her car. She looked at him dressed in casual slacks, an open-collared shirt, and black-leather jacket.

"I left a Christmas gift for you at your condo, but you'll have to hunt for it." He flashed her one of his brilliant smiles and said, "Think of me when you find it."

Maddie reached her hand to hold him, and Giorgio bent

so he could kiss her. She giggled at him. "I hid a gift for you in your suitcase."

They both laughed, and then Giorgio had to leave. "Don't wait for me to take off. Go home. Be safe, *vita mia.*"

"Safe travels." *My very own winemaker.*

CHAPTER 9

The next week, Maddie flew to Maui with her family. The casual, carefree mood of the island always relaxed her. She enjoyed exploring the lava caves and walking through the lava tubes, and the black sand beach in Hana was always a fun excursion. At her hotel, she surfed in the mornings and sometimes rode in the afternoons. Her evenings were spent with her family having dinner and then sitting in the living room while Charlotte played on the floor.

One late afternoon, she received a text from Kai, a friend who lived on the island. Hey, gorgeous. Are you in Maui?

She texted back, Yes.

The reply came through almost instantly, Come over. I'm home.

Okay, be there soon.

MADDIE SAT up on the couch, her balled fists pushing at Kai's chest. They had the only type of relationship Maddie had allowed herself to have—a casual sex relationship. Whenever she was in Maui, and he was free, they would hook up. Kai moved from her, and she pulled her blouse together over her red-lace bra. *What just happened? I don't want this.*

The man next to her broke into her thoughts. "Hey, babe, what's up?"

"I'm sorry. I shouldn't have come here." She stood, tucking her blouse into her linen shorts. "I… I don't… feel… good. I have to go." Maddie grabbed her purse, slinging it over her shoulder.

"If you're not well, let me take you—" She heard the concern in his voice.

"No. Please, I'm so sorry, Kai." She hurried out the door and down the hall to the elevator, taking in deep breaths as she went.

She jabbed at the down button. After what seemed like an eternity, the doors silently opened. Maddie rode the elevator to the garage level. Rushing to her rental car and sliding into the driver's seat, she gripped the steering wheel. Even in the dim light of the garage, she saw her knuckles were white. She rested her forehead on the steering wheel. *Oh God, Giorgio. I want you. I want you and no other man. How did this happen? When did this happen?*

Taking a breath to compose herself, she turned the key in the ignition, backed out of the parking space, and drove to her hotel. *I don't want to care about him or any man. It's just biology. I have to remember that.*

Maddie rushed into her room and picked up the phone. "Room service, please." Maddie waited. "Can you send up a bottle of Chianti and two peaches? No, that's all. Thanks. Yes, just one glass."

She was reeling from what had just happened. While Kai kissed her, all she could think of was Giorgio. She wanted to feel *his* lips, *his* hands, *his* body. Not Kai's. She was an emotional wreck and needed to get back in control. *I won't open myself to hurt again!* All those years in Tokyo, she had focused on work. Work and the infrequent, casual pickup. She would have to get back to that, but this time *only* work.

It wasn't Doug and Nancy's betrayal, or the humiliation she suffered. No. It was how vulnerable love had made her. Nancy had snickered at her for being so blindly in love with Doug. So much so, Maddie didn't realize Doug was using her to advance his career. It was Nancy who he loved. Nancy had laughed, telling her that Doug and she had been secretly seeing each other right under Maddie's nose.

She thought of Giorgio. Tomorrow would be Christmas Eve. The last time she'd spoken with him, he'd sounded distracted—more than that, agitated. No, actually furious. She'd pressed him to tell her what was wrong. Giorgio had said that his mother had been causing trouble again.

"Remember when I told you how my mother treated my grandmother?"

"Yes, you said she wouldn't let her see your father on his death bed, and how the poor woman had to stay at a hotel to be near the hospital."

"What she has done now is a million times worse."

"Oh, Giorgio, I'm so sorry."

Giorgio had said that he didn't want to talk about his mother on the phone. "We can talk when we meet. Perhaps by then, I will have better news."

Maddie knew from Giorgio that Angela was always causing trouble with his family. Giorgio had confided that he didn't have too many good memories of their life after his father had died. His mother wouldn't let him visit his grandmother. Giorgio would have to sneak to the vineyard and villa he now owned to visit her. His Uncle Giuseppe DiMarco encouraged Giorgio to go to Harvard and prepared him to join DiMarco Enterprises.

The knock at the door startled her out of her thoughts. "Room service," a woman's muffled voice called.

Maddie opened the door and moved out of the way to allow her to wheel in the cart with an ice bucket, the wine she had ordered, one glass, and a vase with red roses. "The roses arrived for you while I was preparing your order."

"Oh, they're absolutely beautiful." She bent to smell the blooms and then rubbed a velvety petal between her thumb and finger.

"There is a card for you. Where shall I put the bouquet?"

"On the side table by the sofa, please. You can put the wine and the fruit out on the balcony."

Maddie signed the receipt, and when the server left, she picked up the card. It read, Counting the days until I see you again. One rose for each day. G.

She knew without counting that there were fourteen—two weeks—was a long time until she met him in Nice. She could have gone to him sooner, but she didn't want to go to his cousin's New Year's Eve wedding. *She hated weddings.*

She strolled out to the balcony, poured some wine into the glass, then cut one of the peaches into the wine. She thought of her Sicilian winemaker and the first time they'd had this dessert at his villa. Peaches in wine. Giorgio had cut a ripe, juicy peach into a wine glass. Then he had filled the glass with a full-bodied red wine. Giorgio had taught her so many things. That Doug was the one with the sexual issues making her feel as if she were inadequate. Giorgio taught her how to care again—something she didn't want.

Maddie reclined on the chaise lounge, watching the sunset over Maui. She glanced down at her platinum and diamond GMT wristwatch, a gift from Giorgio. He'd had it set to LA and Sicily time. A smile tugged at her lips. He'd hidden the blue box that was tied with a white satin bow inside an inlaid chestnut wood jewelry box. She'd found it on her dresser when she returned home from dropping him off at the airport. When she'd lifted the lid on the wooden box, a familiar tune had played. One he'd sung to her.

She sighed, *Twelve-hour time difference from Hawaii. Okay, I can text him.* It was early morning in Palermo.

Thank you for the flowers. I love them.

Should she ask about his mother? Though she wanted a casual, no strings attached, no commitment relationship with him, he was doing everything he could to turn this into more. Her heart skipped a beat as she realized that maybe… she didn't mind that.

After her reaction to Kai, she thought rationally. Although it didn't bother her to have casual sex, she could possibly want more than that with Giorgio. More definitely yes, but no commitments or false promises of undying love. None of that for her ever again!

On Christmas Eve morning, she surfed with her brother at the hotel's private beach. Alison didn't want to go surfing, so she sat on a chaise lounge under a straw umbrella, sipping lemonade as she watched them.

"Are you feeling well?" Maddie had asked.

"Yes, I'm just a little nauseous."

"Nauseous? Something you ate?"

Alison smiled at Maddie, then looked at Michael, who said, "We're pregnant. But we were waiting until tonight to tell Mom and Dad."

"OMG! How wonderful. I can't believe it." Maddie clapped her hands together. "Yay, another baby! Since you're not up to surfing, why don't we do something else? The hotel has that beautiful walking trail," Maddie said.

Michael turned to his wife and said, "Do you feel up to that, honey?"

"Yes, that sounds like fun. I can get some exercise in."

"Let's meet in forty-five minutes. I'll shower and meet you by the entrance to the trail."

"Okay. Charlotte, Mom, and Dad are at the pool. Then we can have lunch with them," Michael added.

Her family would stay in Maui through the new year, but Maddie would be going home the day after Christmas. She planned on spending the week between Christmas and New Year going to her office. The bank wouldn't be busy at this time of year, and there were some matters she had to attend to. Client portfolios needed tweaking and such. Traci and Bob had gone skiing in Utah. Traci had mentioned that Doug and Nancy would be in Paris, trying to salvage their marriage.

One day, she woke up extra early and drove to the stable in Santa Barbara. She stopped at a grocery store and bought carrots and apples, enough for all the horses boarded there. The owner of the stable had decorated the barn for the holidays. Each stall had a fresh pine wreath with a red bow. Strung along the breezeway were fresh pine boughs, and sweet-smelling hay covered the floor.

Maddie rode Sir Prance A Lot, and then she spent extra time grooming him. Perched on a stool in his stall, she fed him the treats she'd brought. A cute little mare in the next stall peeked her head over and whickered at Maddie. "Would you like an apple, Missy?"

Sir Prance A Lot pawed the floor, and Maddie said, "He wants to share his treats with you." She fed the mare an apple to munch on.

That night, there would be a party in the barn for all of the owners who boarded their horses there. She didn't want to attend. She wanted no personal life other than spending time with her family. That was the way her heart would remain safe. She gave Sir Prance A Lot extra hugs and kisses before driving back home.

IT WAS the thirty-first of December, and Maddie sat alone on the deck of her condo, watching the surf on Malibu Beach. She was alone by choice. For the past five years, Maddie preferred to be by herself at midnight. When she lived in Tokyo, she would just sleep through to the morning and then call her parents. This year, she could have been with Giorgio at Gianni's wedding, but she really did hate weddings. She couldn't help herself; she just did.

Did she want to meet Giorgio's family? If she were honest, then she didn't know one way or the other. She didn't want any commitment and certainly no more lies. Maddie had bent her no dating rule enough for him.

Her phone pinged, signaling a text from Giorgio; she had given his number a distinctive ringtone. Glancing at the screen, she read the text message.

Want to FaceTime? It's almost midnight here.

She began her text, Yes, but isn't there someone else you — she deleted that and just texted back, Yes.

Maddie waited for the screen to come alive with Giorgio's handsome face. He was in a tuxedo and looking more handsome than ever.

"Happy New Year, *vita mia.*" My life. He'd begun calling her by that endearment the last time they were together at her condo, and when he had kissed her goodbye before boarding his jet.

She said, "Buon Anno."

He grinned. "Have you been learning Italian?"

"Just a little. How was the wedding?"

"Gianni and Sofia have been waiting for this day since they were five years old. I wish you were here."

She heard 10… 9… 8… in Italian.

"Put your lips closer to the screen. I want to kiss you at midnight," he said.

She did, and to her surprise, a tear slid down her cheek.

"If only these miles weren't between us," Giorgio said. "I would take you in my arms and hold you through the night—"

"Oh, just hold me?"

He groaned. "Now I have a hard-on with no relief until next week when we see each other. Then I will—"

"Oh, Giorgio, I miss you too." The words were out—jarring her—before she realized what she'd said. Maddie held her breath, striving to hide her reaction. *Did I just say that? I miss the sex, that's all.* She stumbled over her thoughts.

On the screen, she watched Giorgio as someone said, *"Buon Anno"* and then good-naturedly slapped Giorgio on the back while a petite, red-haired woman handed him a glass of champagne. "For you. Happy New Year, Giorgio."

"Thanks, Liz, and a Happy New Year to you," Giorgio said and kissed her on both cheeks, then he shook the man's hand, saying, "Buon Anno."

"That's my cousin Ricardo and his wife Liz." They walked away, and then Giorgio said, "Next week, when we're together, you and I will have our own special toast."

Maddie composed herself. "Yes, that will be perfect. We'll have a private celebration. Just the two of us."

A WEEK LATER, Giorgio waited for Maddie in France at the Nice airport. Maddie had never been to the French Riviera. Giorgio had teased her, saying, "My SoCal girl needs to bring a heavier coat and warm clothes when we meet."

"It does get cold in Tokyo, so I think I can handle it. I have some warmer clothes."

Giorgio had arrived a few days before so he could meet with his vintner at the Nice vineyard. This past harvest was a disappointment, and Giorgio was concerned. The vines were dormant at this time and needed to be pruned better than they'd been last year. He had walked through the vineyard with his viticulturist, pointing out where it was necessary to cut the old cane so that the next harvest would be as productive as in previous years.

Between this and his concern for his mother, Giorgio had hoped to spend a little extra time with Maddie. He would be flying her back to LA and spend a few days there before he continued on to NY and the board meeting for DiMarco Enterprises.

The news he'd learned from Ricardo was disturbing, to say the least. His mother, with her twisted way of thinking, had almost destroyed Ricardo and his new wife. Because of his mother's diabolical plan, Ricardo didn't know he had a son. Not until he saw Liz again by chance, working in a Fifth Avenue jewelry store did he find out that her son Tony was his son.

His mother hadn't come to the Christmas celebrations nor Gianni's wedding. He'd received a strange text message from her. I'm good and want to be left alone. Let me be and when I feel that I can talk to you, I will come home.

Her phone had been turned off, her townhome in Palermo neat and tidy, but she wasn't anywhere to be found. So, Giorgio had left her to her own crazy behavior. His mother had embroiled an acquaintance of his, Andre Bourbon, into her insane scheme. Giorgio had to ignore his mother and continue with his business and his life. In the middle of all this chaos, Madeline Watson was a breath of fresh air.

In the beginning, he had wanted nothing more than the free and casual sex relationship that Maddie wanted. Now, that had changed. He couldn't think of her with anyone but him. He planned a romantic getaway for her. When they FaceTime'd on New Year's Eve and he saw the tear slide down her cheek, his heart wrenched in his chest. He knew without a doubt that he wanted to always be with her, marry her, keep her safe and happy, have children together. She was his life. *Vita mia.*

He had bought her a ring! That was something he never thought he would do for any woman. Giorgio didn't want a traditional engagement ring. Madeline was anything but conventional. He'd called his old friend Marco whose father owned one of the largest jewelry stores in the world that specialized in rare diamonds, knowing he wanted a pink diamond for her.

The plane arrived on time, and Giorgio picked Maddie up in his Lamborghini. The hotel had provided a car to bring her luggage. She looked beautiful as she walked toward him, her sun-kissed, blonde hair loose and flowing around her shoulders. She wore dark-grey slacks with a lighter-grey-silk blouse and a pink-silk scarf around her neck. Draped around her shoulders, her full-length white cashmere coat and as usual, her stilettos. She was the sexiest woman he had ever seen, and his thought was, *she's here for me.*

"I have missed you," he breathed as he bent to kiss her luscious, pink-tinted lips. Her flowery scent filled his head. He'd had his landscapers plant jasmine in the garden at his villa and also at the Napa vineyard. Now, he thought to have some at each of his vineyards. "How was the flight?"

"Long," she moaned. "But maybe because I missed you and couldn't wait to see you."

He held her slight curves to his side. "Then we had better hurry to the hotel." He whispered, "I can't wait to be in you, and I don't want to embarrass both of us by dragging you into a dark corner."

She gazed up at him. Her moss-green eyes held a spark of mischief as she said, "Really. Can we?"

"Oh, now you tease me." In a more serious tone, he asked, "Are you wearing panties?"

"For the flight? Yes!"

He muttered, "We will be at the hotel in ten minutes."

Her husky laugh shot into his groin. They walked out of the terminal, and he led her to his car. Giorgio held the passenger door open for her. "I thought you flew here."

"I did. This one is exactly like the one at home. I keep this car in the cargo hold of my plane."

She furrowed her brows and said, "I thought you were joking about that." She giggled, shaking her head. "You have a travel Lamborghini!"

He smiled and shrugged a shoulder before he got behind the wheel of his car and turned the ignition.

"I can wait ten minutes but not too much more," she said in a husky voice as she reached her hand over and caressed his crotch. "So nice… Hurry."

Giorgio was so hard by the time they reached the room, he took a step in and then slipped her coat off her shoulders, dropping it on to a chair.

She ran ahead of him. "Is this the bedroom?" Maddie didn't wait for his reply as she opened the door. Her blouse came off and fell to the floor. He toed off his shoes and pulled off his socks. She slipped off her shoes and then did the sexiest hip gyrations out of her pants. Maddie turned to him in her blue-lace bra and the skimpiest thong he had ever seen.

With a trace of laughter, she said, "You're still dressed."

He unzipped his fly and dropped his pants and silk boxers. He watched as her eyes widened. "Oh, yes. I'm hungry for a taste of you."

He groaned, "*Dio*, get on the bed."

"No." She glanced around the room. "The chair... please. You sit in the chair."

He was hard with arousal, and thinking of her lips, her mouth on him, he grew harder. Giorgio tugged his shirt off as blood pounded through his veins, but before he sat in the upholstered accent chair, he pulled Maddie to him. He kissed her full lips, his tongue sliding into her mouth. He'd missed her taste.

She playfully pushed at his shoulders for him to sit in the chair. Maddie dropped to her knees between his feet. She hadn't touched him, and Giorgio prayed he didn't embarrass himself. Maddie gazed into his eyes as her small hands skimmed along his thighs, pressing on his knees to spread them.

She moistened her lips and moved her head toward his erection. "Ahhh," she breathed.

Giorgio bit back a moan. To be held in her sweet mouth was heaven. He did groan as she touched her tongue to him. Her slim fingers held his dick, and she took him into her mouth.

The heat of her mouth almost undid him. His fingers knotted in her silky hair. When her tongue stroked the underside of his dick, he knew he would have to stop her soon. The sweet suction of her mouth.

Dio mio. He stroked her hair, touching her cheek. "*Vita mia,* on the bed. Now, please." He held her shoulders.

"I've dreamt of this," she said in a husky whisper as she rose to her feet, her long, blonde hair cascading down her back. His hand tangled in the locks, rubbing a thick curl between his fingers.

CHAPTER 10

Giorgio led her to the bed. "I have hungered for you, coming into your tight, wet heat."

She swayed toward him. Her pink nipples pressing against sheer, see-through cups of the sexy bra. The tuft of her blonde curls wet the scrap of her matching see-through thong. His mouth dried, gazing at her. He needed to quench his thirst in her body. She stood by the bed, and he unhooked her bra, kissing each nipple before he knelt and pulled her to him.

"You smell like my favorite dessert," he said against her before he licked her through the thong.

She frowned. "What dessert is that?"

"Madeline Watson," he said and slipped the elastic down to her knees. He tugged her to his mouth.

"Oh, Giorgio."

Her moan filled his head. *Just a taste.* He sank his tongue into Maddie's sweet core. His hands roamed up her legs, dragging her to him. Her small hands rested on his head, then her fingers pressed him to her. He opened her wider to lick her glistening flesh, sucking on her sensitive skin.

"Please," she panted. "The... bed."

He rose and laid Maddie on the silky sheets, dragging her thong off her legs. Maddie dug her nails into his shoulders, opening her thighs. She held his throbbing erection and guided him to her heat. He kissed her mouth and sank into a scalding inferno. She held him in her body.

Cupping a breast in his hand, her nipple dug into his palm, and she wrapped her legs around his waist, arching her back. She was beautiful in her desire, driving him on. Giorgio lifted her onto his thighs, pumping into her tight heat. Maddie's head fell forward, her hair in a tangle draped over his shoulder, and she buried her face in his neck.

"Yes, yes, deeper... oh... Ohhhh."

"*Si, vita mia*. Come."

She held onto his shoulders. Her head fell back, and her neck exposed to his lips. He thrust into her and all at once, his own orgasm rushed through him. She shuddered around him, and he filled her, emptying himself into her glorious body.

The soft glow from the lamps on the night tables bathed the room in yellow light. She lay half on top of him. Her head in the crook of his neck while her fingers danced along his ribs and down to his waist. Giorgio's blood pulsed through him.

"I thought we could go out for dinner. We're about fifteen miles from the Italian border, and I like Italian." He held her, skimming his hands down her satin-smooth back, feeling each vertebra as her breasts pressed into his chest.

"I like Italian too." She kissed his neck. Her hands drove him crazy. She leaned into him, sliding one leg over his abdomen. "Especially Sicilian."

"I see we're not talking about food," he said, glancing at her.

She wrapped her fingers around his erection. Maddie stroked him once, twice.

"Ahh, *vita mia*." He lifted her to straddle him. "Take me into the heat of your sweet body."

Her moss-green gaze blazed at him as she eased down his length. Her tight, wet passage surrounding him, setting his blood on fire.

They eventually got to the restaurant in Bordighera on the Italian Riviera. Maddie's long tresses shone with streaks of gold in the candle flame. Her cheeks were rosy from their earlier lovemaking. And her lips—swollen from his kisses. She bit into a piece of lobster ravioli, chewed, and then drank some wine.

"How old was your mother when you were born?" She surprised him with her question.

They had touched on the subject of his mother earlier. He leaned back in his seat and said, "She had just turned sixteen."

"Wow. I didn't realize she was that young. Was that even legal?"

Giorgio chuckled. "It is different here."

"Your mother was so young when she had you and then to lose her husband. What was she, twenty-four?"

He nodded and sipped his wine.

Maddie said, "She must have been devastated, and… maybe being near your grandmother… made the pain worse for her. The house must have held too many memories of a happier time."

Giorgio stroked Maddie's fingers. *She has a better understanding of the situation than I ever did.* "I know she was young, and it was better for us to live in Palermo, near my uncle and his family. That doesn't excuse her behavior. To cause all of this trouble now. How long was she planning this and why?"

Maddie glanced at him, and he saw empathy in the moss-green depths. "That's a question only your mother knows the answer to. But Giorgio… she may not even know the reason."

"Enough of my mother. Do you want more wine?"

Maddie patted her stomach. "No, I'm stuffed."

"Then let's go."

They arrived back at the hotel, and Giorgio handed his car keys over to the valet.

"We can stroll along the pathway overlooking the water," Giorgio said to Maddie.

They walked on the lighted path down to the edge where the sandy beach began. The moon cast a silver glow on the Mediterranean. The gentle waves of the surf and the sea breeze added to the mood of the night. Giorgio took her small hand in his. Turning it palm up, he placed a kiss in the center.

"Tomorrow, we can drive to Monaco. Take in some of the sights and just have a pleasant day."

She leaned against him, resting her head on his chest, and said, "Do we have to get up very early?"

He hugged her into his body, breathing in the flowery scent of her hair as he said, "Hmm, I see a pattern here. You like to sleep in and laze around in bed." He kissed the top of her head.

"I have developed that desire… recently," she said.

"Well, then we can order breakfast in bed before we go." He touched her temple with his lips and couldn't resist running the tip of his tongue along the shell of her ear and whispering, "Let's get a head start right now, lazing in bed."

The next day, they did have breakfast in bed. Then they drove to Monaco. Driving along the winding road over-looking the Mediterranean, the sun sparkled on the water, turning the sea to thousands of winking diamonds.

Giorgio took her to the world-famous casino in Monte Carlo. He held elite member status, and although he wouldn't gamble, he wanted to show Maddie the extraordinary architecture. Giorgio stopped his Lamborghini at the main entrance of the casino, and a valet approached. *"Bonjour, Signor* Lombardo."

"Bonjour," Giorgio replied. "We would like to go in for a brief time."

"Qui Mosiure, anything you wish." The valet opened Giorgio's door.

Giorgio walked around to open the car door for Maddie. "We can go in, and I will show you the grandeur of the main salon, the casino, and the attached opera house."

"Do you come here often? They know you by name."

"No, not often. You know that occasionally business must be conducted while entertaining."

"Yes, I guess that's true. My family likes Las Vegas. We haven't been there in ages though."

Then he drove to another of Monte Carlo's exclusive neighborhoods. He parked his Lamborghini, and they walked along the streets, coming to the grounds of the prince's palace, which overlooked the main harbor. The port was full of yachts, and anchored further out were super yachts and two cruise ships.

"I think one of DiMarco Enterprises' Contessa Line cruise ships is in port. Would you like to have lunch on board with the captain?"

"Is that possible?"

"Yes. I am on the board of directors, and we can go onto the ship if you like."

She smiled up at him and pressed her lethal body against his. Her hand resting on his chest, she said, "Actually, I remember reading that you are the chairman of *that* board."

Wrapping his arms around her tiny waist, he kissed her sweet lips. He loved the interest she took in him. Not like most of the women he knew. The minute they found out there was DiMarco money running through his veins, they were all over him. They were happier with his wallet than him. Willing to give him what they thought he wanted from them, oral sex. They were happy to kneel before him and take him into their mouths.

He took out his phone, scrolled through his contacts, and called the ship. A motorboat met them at the dock and brought them out to where the ship was anchored. They had lunch on board with the captain, a jovial older man. Then they stayed on board until the ship was ready to sail.

Back at the hotel, Maddie walked into the room and just as Giorgio closed the door behind them, she reached for him.

"Kiss me," she sighed. "I had a great day but now—"

His lips cut off whatever she was going to say. In seconds, he had removed her clothes, kissing each part of her seductive body as he stripped her. Kneeling before Maddie, he lifted his hands to the gentle curve of her hips, tugging her to his mouth, needing a taste. He inhaled her sweet scent.

Her fingers reached into his hair, and Maddie caressed his head. His groin throbbed as his tongue teased the tuft of blonde curls parting her seam. He stroked his hands along her hips to the satin skin of her firm buttocks. Pulling her forward, he thrust his tongue deep into her core, licking her, tasting her wild arousal.

Giorgio caressed the back of one leg, and holding her knee, he guided her thigh over his shoulder. Her moan filled his ears as her hands gripped him. He licked and teased her. Opening her, circling her clit with his tongue. Maddie moved her hips forward, and he sheathed his tongue in her, licking the walls of her vagina. The pressure of her fingers in his hair and the movement of her hips told him she was about to come. He held her to his mouth, thrusting his tongue into her over and over again.

"Oh, Giorgio, suck… my clit."

He did.

"Ahhh, ahh, yes. God, yes… so good."

He nudged her forward, reaching deeper into her. Her taste on his tongue held him, and he lashed at her sensitive clit before thrusting into her core.

"Oh God, oh God, ahh… ahh." She pressed closer, shuddering. Pulse after pulse, she climaxed.

Giorgio caught Maddie in his arms and carried her to the bed. She opened her eyes, and the burn of desire he saw in the depths inflamed him.

She whispered, "My turn."

"No. Not yet. Soon. But right now… I need to be in you." He dropped his pants to the floor and gazed into her moss-green eyes. "See how ready I am?"

"Oh, yes, come here." Maddie scooted to the center of the bed, her arms outstretched for him. They spent the rest of that day and most of the next day in bed.

MADDIE SAT IN A PINK, sleeveless sheath dress on the plush sofa in their hotel living room. They'd spent almost twenty-four hours in bed having the best sex—as always—with him. Giorgio had dressed in casual, navy slacks that hugged his narrow waist and a light-blue, button-down shirt. The first three buttons were open, dark chest hair peeking through, and his sleeves were rolled up to his elbows.

He'd received an unexpected call from his Nice vintner and needed to discuss the results of the soil report that had been ordered. He paced the length of the living room in his Italian loafers.

She curled her legs under her and closed her eyes, listening to his sexy voice as he spoke in fluent French. Her high school French was rusty at best, but she didn't want to eavesdrop on his conversation. When he ended the call, he came and sat next to her.

She opened her eyes and glanced into his intense aqua gaze. "This is our time, no more business. I don't want any further interruptions." He stretched his arm around her shoulders and snuggled her to his side. "I would like to talk with you."

Her stomach clenched. "Talk about what?" her voice broke. *Talking meant relationship, and a commitment. Exactly what I don't want. I knew I shouldn't have asked about his mother or taken an interest in his family. No. No. No. Big mistake. I won't do that again.*

Giorgio took her out more and more as if they were on dates. No longer simply meeting for long weekend getaways to have sex. Even sightseeing in Monaco and lunch on the cruise ship yesterday was clearly a date. He would take her dancing or out to dinner, talking about his life and recently about how much he missed her when she was in LA. He'd begun to take an interest in her work and career. Asking her if she missed Japan.

She'd told him of her restlessness, but also needing to be near her family. He'd suggested that perhaps she should become a consultant for Watson Financial, do more of the things she loved, such as working in loss mitigation and real estate. He'd gone so far as suggesting that she could help him find the next vineyard for Lombardo Wines.

"I hope you want the same things I want. A deeper relationship and a commitment that we will—"

Her heart pounded. "I can't. I can't do this." She broke out in a cold sweat. "Not after Doug… I won't. I mean…" Her leg muscles tightened. *I'm so confused.*

"I am not your ex, nor can you compare me to that weak-minded incompetent. He didn't know how lucky he was to have the love of a woman like you. I am *not* him."

"I know, Giorgio. I know we've skirted the issue. For a long time, I've known that what we have isn't just sex. Though I've tried to put it into a neat little basket to take out when I felt the desire. I never wanted to hurt you, but... I... I *can't*."

"Okay, let's not think about that. You know my feelings. Since the day I met you, there has been no other in my life... or... my bed. Only you. You are all I want, *vita mia*."

She groaned at his words. Then she bowed her head, unable to look at him. "I don't think there is happy ever after for me... *Not* anymore."

He scrubbed his fingers through his hair, and his voice held a note of his frustration with her. "Because you won't give yourself a chance." He stood and strode to the window, then he turned to her. "Don't you know?" He poked his finger into his chest. "I am your happy ever after. Me. Giorgio Lombardo. *I* am your destiny."

She clenched her jaw and shook her head. *No!* She couldn't trust her heart. She had to protect herself from hurt. "No!" She stood. "We meet. We have sex. Then you go your way, and I go mine. We have separate lives. No commitment. That's the way *I* want it." With her hands on her hips, she almost stamped her foot. "Why must you change things?"

She didn't look at him; her eyes darted around the room. She spun around. The walls were closing in on her; she couldn't take a deep enough breath. Maddie hurried to the closet and yanked her coat from the hanger. "I have to go. I can't talk about this anymore." She shoved her arms into the sleeves.

Giorgio shouted, "I hate what he did to you. I hate how he hurt you." His voice thundered around her. "Don't walk away from what we have. You know it's more than sex." His voice dropped, *"I love you."*

Fear gripped at her stomach, and her brain screamed.

Run. "I can't see you anymore." Her voice was a panicked whisper.

She picked up her purse and ran from the room and down the hall. Ignoring the elevator, she hurried down the steps and out of the hotel. Out front, Maddie didn't wait for the doorman to hail a taxi. She jumped into the first one in line.

In rusty French, she said, "Take me to the airport, international flights." She left her suitcase, everything behind. In the back of the cab, she had to think—no, just leave him. *The nerve of him to say he loved me. Forget him. Go back home and bury yourself in work, the same as you did before.*

At the ticket counter, she waited briefly for her turn. "When is the next flight to Los Angeles?"

The ticket agent looked at her screen and pressed some keys before she said, "You just missed the five p.m. They've pulled away from the gate. It was the last flight for this evening."

The agent looked down at her screen again and typed. Then typed some more. She looked up at Maddie, and with a smile, said, "There's one seat left on the next flight at six thirty tomorrow morning. It has a forty-five-minute stop in Munich, but you won't have to change planes."

"I'll take it." She opened her purse. "Oh," Maddie huffed, "I forgot my phone. Well, it's okay. I'm not going back to the hotel for it." *I'll buy a new one when I get home.*

"May I see your identification and your passport, miss?" Maddie handed over the documents, and the ticket agent input the information on her keyboard, then she asked, "Ms. Watson, do you have any luggage to check?"

"No. No luggage." She handed her credit card to the agent. *I left everything behind. I'll have my things shipped back to me.*

Maddie sat in a metal airline seat at the terminal, numb to

what had happened. She had walked out on him. Why did he have to *change* things? Exclusivity was good, she had realized that at Christmas, in Maui when Kai touched her, but all she craved was Giorgio. But why more than that? *Why drag my heart into this?* Why? Her shoulders sagged. The lump in her throat grew, and her mouth was dry as if she'd eaten sand. Sitting there for how long she didn't know. She had left her wristwatch along with her phone at the hotel. She looked around, her gaze pausing on the monitor with the various flights' departure times on it.

She was back at the ticket counter. "I've changed my mind. I won't need that seat."

Then she hailed a cab. "Take me to Cap-De Louis hotel."

The ride back to the hotel took more time than the trip to the airport. It was eleven p.m., and the lobby of the grand hotel was virtually empty. When she entered, the concierge called to her, "Miss Watson." Maddie walked across the white marble and black granite floor over to the reception desk.

"Mr. Lombardo has checked out. I have placed your belongings in the baggage room for safekeeping."

She felt nauseous, the lobby spun. A pain stabbed her chest. "Th… thank you." Maddie squared her shoulders and stood tall. "By chance, did Mr. Lombardo leave my phone?"

"Oh yes, Madame, excuse me. I have placed that into the hotel safe. I will be but a moment." The concierge went behind the desk and through a wrought-iron, scrolled gate into the back room.

Giorgio… had gone… He… left… me. She was distraught. *You brought this on yourself.* She couldn't treat him in such a way and expect him to stay.

"Here, Madame, is your phone, and in the cotton pouch is your wristwatch. Shall I prepare a room for you?"

"No, thank you. Did Mr. Lombardo leave a message for me?"

"I'm sorry. No, he did not. He did say that he was going home to Palermo and to forward any communications for him there."

"Thank you. I would like a taxi to the airport." How she managed to get those words out without crying, she wasn't sure.

"Please have a seat." He directed her to a secluded seating area with four wing chairs arranged around a glass-topped pedestal table. "Would you like a beverage and a light snack?"

"No, thank you," her voice cracked.

"I will call the bellman to bring out your luggage, and I will have one of the hotel limousines take you wherever you wish to go."

Maddie sat in the opulent lobby of the grand hotel. Her shoulders drooped. *Why couldn't he leave well enough alone? He said he loves me... and then... he walks out on me. He's just like Doug.* She sighed. *I ran away from Giorgio. What did I expect? I ran rather than talk to him and tell him my feelings.* She groaned. *Giorgio is different; he's not Doug.* "I love him."

What? I... love... him? Maddie held her breath for a moment as her thoughts collided. Leaning back in the chair, she massaged her temple. *I... love... him!* With trembling fingers, she turned on her phone and texted Giorgio. I was wrong. Please forgive me. She bit her bottom lip, and then she tapped send.

Two heartbeats later, her phone rang. "Hello," she whispered in a broken voice.

"Where are you?" His voice sounded gruff.

Her throat was tight, holding back tears. She managed to say, "At the hotel."

"Don't leave. I will be there shortly." Through the phone, she heard the motor of his car revving and tires spinning.

"I won't." Tears stung her eyes.

Minutes after she ended the call, the concierge walked

over to her. "Madame, Mr. Lombardo has ordered the presidential suite. I will be happy to escort you and have your luggage brought up."

By the time she had settled in the suite, Giorgio burst into the room. Tie askew, hair mussed. He stood just inside the door. She ran to him. Giorgio lifted her into his arms, holding her off the floor. His lips trailed fire from her throat to her lips. His mouth possessed hers, hot and demanding. Liquid fire flooded her core.

His big hands tugged at her, pulling her against his hard body, into arms of steel. He held her to him. Maddie slipped his tie from his neck. She pulled his shirttails out of his pants, unbuttoned the shirt, and ran her hands up to his chest. Their mouths were fused together, tongues clashing, circling.

They stood just inside the closed door. Giorgio leaned her against the wall. His hand reached for her leg, caressing it as he lifted the hem of her dress up around her waist. He reached into the elastic of her panties. His long fingers touched her mound, before sliding into her center. He grunted, then he ripped the delicate lace.

She held back a moan and unzipped his pants. Reaching into his silk boxers, her fingers wrapped around his steel-encased, huge erection. Then she hitched a leg up his side.

Giorgio pressed her against the wall. He slipped his arm under her leg and trapped her knee in the crook of his elbow. Shifting to hold her, he slipped his other arm under her other knee in the same sexy way. She held on to him, her arms around his neck.

He was at her entrance, hard and hot. His lips never leaving hers, his tongue filled her mouth as the fury of his deep thrust filled her. She sucked on his tongue. Not willing to give him complete power over her, Maddie wrapped her arms tighter around Giorgio's neck. The wall at her back held her so she could get a better grip. She rubbed her breasts against his chest; the fabric of her dress excited her nipples.

Giorgio kept her impaled on his magnificent male length. Harder, faster, she grasped his shoulders, her nails digging into his skin, holding him to her, hot and wild. Needing his strength and the deep thrusts of his possession. It was over in minutes as liquid fire streamed through her, and the shuddering waves of her orgasm consumed her.

He exploded into her. She clung to him as they both gasped for breath. Maddie rested her head on his shoulder. His breathing heavy, her lips against the damp crook of his neck, she kissed him, and his scent filled her head as she clung to his strong body. He moved his arm, and she wrapped her leg around his waist. She locked her ankles while he held her buttocks in his cupped hands and walked into the bedroom. With one hand, he pulled the bedspread from the bed and eased her to sit on the edge of the mattress. Her eyes opened to see him as he toed his shoes off and dropped his pants. She started to unzip her dress.

"Don't. I want to strip you." He shrugged out of his shirt. Then he knelt on one knee to slip her shoes from her feet. His long fingers stroked up her calf, over her leg, between her thighs.

"Giorgio…"

"Si, Maddalena." He slipped her thigh-high nylons down and off. He stood and unzipped her dress, sliding the pink fabric down her arms.

"Hold on to me." Giorgio wrapped one powerful arm around her waist and lifted her from the mattress just enough to let her dress glide to the floor.

He slipped the straps of her lacy bra down her arms, kissing the crests of her breasts, sliding his tongue into the valley as he reached around her to unhook the bra.

He stopped long enough to nip at her breast before he

sucked a turgid nipple into his hot mouth. Then he brushed what was left of her panties from her body. "Lie back on the bed." His aqua-blue eyes smoldered with desire.

A new wave of excitement flowed through her, and she scooted to lie against the pillows, watching him. He was a mass of rippling muscle, and he was hard again. His massive erection was coated with her orgasm.

He was ready for her again. Giorgio lay on top of Maddie, covering her with his marble-hard, beautiful body. She welcomed his weight and his arms surrounding her. He spread her legs with his knees and with one sure thrust, he embedded himself into her heat. He rose up on his arms and locked his elbows, going deeper.

"Please don't ever walk away from me again. We can work through anything. It can be whatever you want. But never leave me."

Maddie slid her palms up his massive pecs and over his broad shoulders. Then lifted her arms around his neck. He unlocked his elbows, lowering himself, his chest pressing her breasts, rubbing her nipples. The friction of his chest hair on her breasts and his deep penetration made Maddie moan as she lifted her hips to him.

This time was slower, and his seductive lips coaxed her to kiss him. He licked her neck, whispering, "Are you ready for make-up sex? I love the sounds you make when you come." He sucked on her nipple.

She lifted her legs and locked her ankles, pressing her heels into his back. "Yes, make me come." His deep strokes pistoned into her again and again. Maddie forgot the world. Only this man who held her mattered.

CHAPTER 11

Confusion seized Maddie. How could she not realize what she felt for Giorgio? Resting her head on the pillow, she turned to gaze at him. He slept so peacefully, lying next to her. One suntanned, muscular arm was thrown over her waist, his knee pressing against her thigh. She shifted, not wanting to wake him. She had been through so much. Doug was the past and not a good one. Giorgio had said he was her future, and that it was more than lust they shared.

She jumped out of the king-size bed, ran into the bathing suite, and turned on the tub spigots. She needed to soak and clear her mind. Running away was no longer an option. She'd been running ever since she moved to Japan. She had to face up to that and stop hiding from her emotions—her fear of being loved.

Once the tub filled, she turned on the spa feature. Silently, the water swirled. She piled her hair in to a messy bun on top of her head and dropped the white velvet hotel robe to the marble floor. She stepped down the three steps into the massive jacuzzi. "Ahh," she sighed.

Sitting on the built-in seat that ran along one side, she

submerged herself to her shoulders, leaning her head back. *I need to relax. Get a perspective on where I'm headed.* Her analytical mind needed to turn off and be more like Giorgio, laidback.

A smile tugged at her lips. Laidback, oh, when he laid back, and she took charge of their lovemaking. She smiled at that thought as her eyes closed. Seeing him in her mind, he stood before her, a naked god. His magnificent erection almost touching his belly, she climbed onto his lap and held back a moan. Her hand—

"You look well-loved."

Keeping her eyes closed, she said, "I am. Yes, I am."

She lifted her head from the rim of the tub and gazed up at the man who turned her world upside down. He was naked just as she'd imagined. He stood tall, his muscles sculpted better than Michelangelo's David. His virility made her core pulse with desire. Would it always be like this? The warmth of the water swirling around her. She lifted an arm. "Come here."

Giorgio sank into the tub and sat next to Maddie. "You look like a Roman goddess, with your cheeks flushed pink. Just like when I make you orgasm."

Excitement tingled through her as his fingers skimmed her back. "You are too far away. Sit on my lap."

"Really... I would love nothing more..." She turned to him.

He held her waist, lifting her over him, and his lips found hers. Opening her mouth to his searing kiss, she lifted one leg over his lap, a knee on either side of his muscular thighs, she straddled him. Their tongues entwined. Her hand slid down between them, into the swirling water. Her fingers closed over his excited flesh. Giorgio lifted her just enough to lick a hard nipple before sucking the whole of it into his mouth.

Her head tipped back as a thrilling zing of desire shot into her core. She was ready, but she'd learned that Giorgio never settled for the easy way, and she would have to beg before he satisfied her. Moving his powerful hands from her waist down to her hips, he slid her up on his massive thighs, capturing her hand and his erection between them.

"Oh, I'm so wet for you." She sighed.

"*Si, vita mia*. The bath water," he teased her mercilessly.

"You think that's what it is? I assure you that isn't what I meant." Her fingers tightened around his granite-hard shaft.

His husky laugh floated around them as he licked her nipples, settling on one to nip at before he sucked the pointed peak into the scorching heat of his mouth. Exciting her other breast, he plucked at her nipple with the pad of his callused thumb and forefinger.

Heat flooded her core, and she lifted herself up to guide him to her entrance. Holding his erection and rubbing the head over her labia, she gazed into his eyes, panting, "Let me show you how ready I am."

Giorgio's aqua eyes ignited. All traces of teasing were gone and replaced by a burning fire. Playtime was over. She sank down his length as he pushed up into her.

"Yes, hot and—"

Maddie tightened her vaginal muscles around his glorious cock.

He groaned, "Strega."

She reached her open palms up onto his stubble-covered cheeks. "No talking. Kiss me," she said and covered his lips with hers, slipping her tongue into his mouth as she rode him.

Water sloshed around them. He tasted so good. She moaned into his mouth as the first waves of her climax began. Giorgio held her waist, and his hands slid to her hips, pulling her into him as he lifted and lowered her on his granite-hard length.

She whimpered, moaning, and then exploded into a million pieces of bliss. Her head rested on his shoulder, breathing in his scent. She kissed droplets of bathwater from his neck. Then she kissed his stubble-covered jaw.

"More?" he whispered.

"Yes. Let's go to that nice comfy bed."

"That's pretty far away… in the other room." He lifted her out of the tub and laid her on the heated marble floor. "Here is better."

She opened her arms to him, and Giorgio spread her knees. Kneeling over her, he kissed her mouth and then her neck, her breasts, her belly, her abdomen. He looked up her body, and she stared into his aqua-blue gaze. A moan of anticipation escaped her.

"Yes, Giorgio."

He smiled and spread her curls to kiss her center. His tongue was magic as he played with her clit before licking into her core. Knees bent, she spread her thighs, reaching for his head. Her fingers slipped in his thick hair, beseeching him. He used his tongue to circle her clitoris before he sucked her folds. She couldn't stay still. Maddie lifted herself to his mouth, writhing and moaning.

Giorgio thrust his tongue into her over and over, driving her to another orgasm. Her muscles tightened, her hips rolled, pushing her pelvis up to his glorious mouth. Her thighs shook. She did scream as the rippling waves of her climax washed over her. Her feet slid along the tile floor, and Maddie caught her breath as the euphoric spell he cast on her subsided. Giorgio's lips moved on her, kissing her center.

"Oh, Giorgio… I'm so…" She couldn't speak.

He pushed her knees up, and then his tongue moved all over her sensitive flesh. He didn't rush her. She was close to another orgasm, unable to hold back her moans. She held his head to her. Giorgio stopped.

"Ohhh," she groaned. Maddie lifted herself to his mouth and yanked his dark hair.

"You have no patience." His lips moved against her wet flesh. "Shall I use my tongue?"

"Yes… and… more."

He held her buttocks, spreading her wider with his thumbs, opening her to his mouth. He sucked her sensitized clit then slid the tip of his tongue around and over the bud, back and forth with just the tip of his tongue over her clit. Her toes curled, and she lifted herself to his mouth. His tongue plunged deep into her center.

Maddie's thighs held his head, and her fingers clenched in his hair to hold him to her. Her back arched, and once more, he sucked her clit before he slowly slid his finger into her.

"Ahh… ummah, oh yes," she moaned.

He thrust once, twice, and she exploded into ecstasy. When her shudders of pleasure stopped, Giorgio gave her a moment, and then he moved a second finger into her. His tongue felt like a caress on her sensitive clit. He used the tip of his tongue to slide back and forth before he flattened it to lick over all of her.

Pleasure consumed her. Her abdomen tightened, and as his fingers found her G-spot, Maddie bit back a whimper, "I'm oh, yes, yes…" He crooked his fingers. "Right there." Her words ended on a moan she couldn't hold back.

He sucked her clit into his mouth, and his tongue ignited a fire in her. Her orgasm, when it came, shook her body. She held his head closer to her, unable to stop herself from grinding against his mouth, as the waves of her orgasm swept over her. He stayed with her, prolonging her pleasure. Slowly, her breathing returned to normal. Giorgio lifted her in his arms, and her body melted into him.

He nuzzled her neck and kissed her lips. "Now, we can go to the bed," he said.

Maddie looped her arms around his strong neck as he carried her. She would always remember Nice.

~

IN THE EARLY MORNING HOURS, Giorgio's phone rang. He cursed in Italian, "I have to take this… It's my mother."

He spoke in his Sicilian dialect. Maddie had taken an interest in learning more than *ciao*, and this was different. She watched him as he spoke. He sat up, muscles bunching as he threw his legs over the side of the bed and stood. Crescent-shaped marks covered his shoulders, and longer scratches ran down his back. Heat rose into her cheeks. *Make-up sex.*

Orgasm upon orgasm, she'd almost forgotten her name!

Giorgio stepped into his pants.

Maddie knew their time together was over. She rose and went into the en suite to take a shower. A short time later, he followed her into the shower.

"I'm sorry about this. I will make it up to you." His strong arms came around her waist, pulling her back against his naked body. Under the gentle spray from the water, he said, "I called and have arranged for a private jet to fly you home. I have to go back to Palermo."

Maddie turned to face him. "No, I can just as easily take a commercial flight. I don't want to fly alone on a big plane. Please, I want to take a regular flight. Besides, I parked my car at LAX."

He held her, kissing her lips as his hands roamed over her body. "I don't want to leave you here."

"You have to see what's wrong with your mother, and

then you have the board meeting in NY. We can meet as we planned next month in Las Vegas. You must go."

"I want to get you settled first."

Maddie had turned on the side panels of the shower, and now the warm water sprayed them. "Just hold me," she said, reaching up on her toes to kiss him. He lifted her, and she was so ready for him to thrust into her. She loved him. Oh God, she loved him.

They made love in the shower and then on the bathroom floor and against the living room wall. She memorized him. His face, his body, yet she continued to fear a commitment. All the bad memories of Doug flooded back. How he never held her after they made love or wanted her to rest her head on his chest. "My arm is falling asleep. Move over, Mad." What she had thought to be normal, Giorgio taught her that it wasn't. Sometimes, she'd just lay on top of Giorgio, naked, and they would talk for hours. He'd told her about his childhood, growing up in Palermo.

She and Giorgio had made it back to the bed. Now, he kissed her brow as she lay across his chest. "Let's get your flight booked and, then once you're on your way, I will go back to Palermo and see to my mother."

Giorgio drove Maddie to the airport and waited with her until her flight was called. He pulled her into his arms. "*Vita mia,* be safe and call me when you arrive home." He kissed her cheek, pulling her closer. "I miss you already," he said then kissed the tip of her nose.

Maddie held him and reached her parted lips up to him. She pressed her luscious soft lips to his. He controlled himself and didn't lift her into his arms. *Don't carry her away.*

"What will you do?"

"Right now, I'm using all my willpower not to take you with me."

She touched his cheek, her eyes glassy. "I meant when I leave."

He breathed in her sweet scent. "My jet is fueled and waiting. I will depart shortly after you. I'll go and see what the 'big' emergency is with my mother. She can be dramatic at times."

He watched a blush stain her cheeks. "You, Maddalena, are not dramatic. You are very levelheaded."

The overhead speaker announced last call for her flight, and Maddie reached up to kiss him one more time. "I have to go. I'll call you when I land." She walked to the boarding gate. Then turned and blew him a kiss.

He stood in the terminal, looking out the window, and waited until her plane pulled away from the gate. An airport attendant approached him, speaking French, "Mr. Lombardo, I am here to escort you to your aircraft at the business terminal. It is cleared for departure as soon as you arrive."

"Good." He walked with the attendant to the waiting limousine. "Your car was taken to your plane by one of your flight crew."

"Yes, I am aware of that. Thank you."

In the back of the limousine, Giorgio slipped his phone from his pocket and texted, I miss you already.

Then he called his mother. "I'm boarding now and should be at your townhome in two hours." His mother had sounded so distraught when she first called him, but now, she sounded calmer. After he ended the call, he texted Maddie again. Be safe, vita mia. Call me when you land.

When his jet touched down at the airport outside of Palermo, Giorgio got into his car and drove directly to his mother's townhome. The three-story stone structure sat at the end of a street with a row of similar homes in an exclusive area of the city. He'd grown up in that house after his father had died. Giorgio thought back to how she would spend hours and hours at his grave and how she'd tried to hide her tears from him. Her face swollen from all the crying —twenty-five years of sadness.

When he arrived, his mother buzzed him in, and he climbed the stairs up to the third-floor living room. She stood on the landing, waiting for him, and hugged him to her. "Oh, Giorgio. I'm sorry to take you away from business, but I needed to talk with you. Come sit in the kitchen. I'll make coffee."

She looked different, and Giorgio couldn't determine what it was. He sat at the kitchen table, and she said to him, "After careful consideration, I will go to the Napa vineyard."

"You couldn't tell me this over the phone? You've been gone for weeks with no contact. You missed Christmas, Gianni's wedding. You sent me that ridiculous text and now—"

"I don't want to stay here any longer," she said. "I needed to talk with you about that and not long distance."

"When you say here, do you mean this house, or Palermo? Are you running away again, Mother? Do you think California is far enough away to forget everything you've done? Where did you go when you disappeared? Your callus behavior—"

"I don't want to talk about it." She moved away from him.

He shook his head and sighed. "After all the trouble you caused, now you don't want to talk about it. Well then, what do you want to talk about?"

"When I arrived home and you were away, I decided to go to my brother Giuseppe to apologize for my terrible behavior to Ricardo."

"And you think that will make it better?"

"It's a start. Although I doubt Ricardo and Liz will ever forgive me, I am sorry for what I did."

"I don't understand how you could be so manipulative and why you thought you had the *right* to meddle in such a malicious way."

He walked over to his mother. She looked so small and sad. He held her to him and sighed. "Mom, I want to help you, but can I trust you not to cause any more trouble?"

Giorgio noticed that her hair was down around her shoulders and not in that *old lady* bun she had worn for years. He held her away from him. "Your hair is different. Like the mother of my youth."

His mother glanced away. "Yes, I have also removed the mourning black that I have worn for twenty-five years."

He looked at her, a smile playing around his lips. "That dress looks pretty black to me."

It was more than the hair; she had an inner glow he'd never noticed before. "I hope you'll stop meddling and causing problems. I want to be clear… I am happy with my life, so I would be extremely upset if you turned your attention to causing trouble for me."

She stepped back and stretched her neck to look at him. "No, Giorgio. You're my son, and I only want the best for you." She patted his hand. "My brother told me you never wanted to become CEO of DiMarco Enterprises. He offered you the opportunity, and you turned it down."

"I told you that years ago. Had you listened to me, you would have known."

"*E*, sometimes mammas think they know best."

He shook his head and sighed. "When do you want to leave for California?"

"Right away. And Giorgio, I don't want anyone to know where I am."

His brows came together. "I know you, Mom. What are

you hiding? I'm sure there is much more you are not telling me."

She shrugged a shoulder and tipped her head. "You always think the worst."

"With good reason. I do feel that you can take charge of the project at the vineyard. It will give you something to do where you can use your managerial skills. I will notify the architect."

"I would like to stop in Milan for a few days, to do some shopping and then go to California. I can go alone. I know you have appointments and obligations. My brother said I can use one of DiMarco Enterprises' jets, so I would like to leave tomorrow."

He kissed his mother and then left her townhouse to drive home to his villa. His mother and Maddie would be the death of him. He missed sleeping with Maddie. Cuddling her to him or when she would roll over and wake him. The corners of his lips rose, remembering how sometimes Maddie would only want to snuggle closer to him in her sleep, and he'd be the one to wake her. He'd never cared for anyone the way he cared for Maddie.

Giorgio glanced at his wristwatch; it was nine in the evening here in Palermo, and Maddie hadn't called yet. He expected a call or at least a text at any moment. It was late afternoon in LA when his phone rang. "Hello, Maddie."

"Hi. My plane just landed, and I'm on my way to my car in the parking garage. I read your texts, and I miss you too… How is your mother?"

"Better than she sounded when she called me, though it was good that I came home. We had a long-overdue talk about a lot of things. She's going to help me with the Napa vineyard."

"That's wonderful. I'm happy that your mother is willing to do that for you."

AFTER FRANCE, they spoke almost every day. One night while they were on FaceTime, Giorgio persuaded her to have a relationship with him that was much more than just sex. She was sitting on the deck of her condo, sipping a glass of wine. "You know you're a better negotiator than I am. You're good at this."

He smiled at her. "I have to win, *vita mia*. You see... I have much more to lose."

She laughed and held up a file. "I have to get these reports ready... Giorgio, I'm going to take your advice and talk to my brother about consulting for Watson Financial."

"Good, I know it will be better for you. You can do what you like, loss mitigation and real estate. Then you can help me find the next vineyard for Lombardo Wines to purchase."

"Oh, I see how it's going to be. I'll free up my time so *you* can monopolize it."

"I want to take up all of your time—but no more talk like that until we see each other, and I can make good on keeping you in my bed," he said.

"Okay... and Giorgio... I love when you keep me in bed, or the shower, or the—"

He groaned, feeling the rush of blood in his groin. "Oh Maddalena, come meet me in Sicily."

She made a pouty face at him that drove him wild. "I have to go. Buona sera for now. We will be in Las Vegas before you know it."

"Si, but not soon enough for me."

CHAPTER 12

Maddie met her mother for lunch in Santa Monica. They'd decided to go to a Chinese restaurant near Watson Financial.

"How's Dad?"

"He's getting stronger each day. I'm happy that he retired. He always worked such long hours, and I never saw him."

"I'm delighted that it's working out for you and Dad. You do know that Michael agreed to my offer. I will consult rather than stay on permanently. It gives me some freedom—"

"Yes. All these long weekends… if I didn't know better, I would think you've met someone."

Maddie averted her eyes.

She heard her mother's quick intake of breath before she exclaimed, "You *have*. Oh, darling, tell me."

Maddie placed her chopsticks on her plate and glanced at her mother, then sighed, "It's still too new… and I… well, please don't push me."

"I won't. But I'm so happy you've finally come to your senses—

"Mother, is this *not* pushing?"

"Okay, no more. I promise, but please don't make me wait too long. All I want is your happiness."

The next day, Maddie drove to Rodeo Drive. Giorgio had said that he wanted them to have a special evening on Valentine's Day and to bring a formal dress. Once she had agreed to a relationship with him, Maddie decided that going out on Valentine's Day would be fun. She usually ignored the day and all its symbols of love. She walked past a boutique, and a dress caught her eye. It wasn't red, and that was great. This one had the thinnest satin straps, with a satin bow across the bodice, hugging the mannequin before layers of pink-ruffled tulle ended at the knee. *It's beautiful.* She walked into the boutique.

A few days later, at LAX, she boarded the plane for the short flight to McCarran International Airport in Las Vegas. Giorgio had booked a penthouse suite at Caesars Palace, the most luxurious hotel on the strip. The suite he'd reserved she knew was one of the most expensive in Las Vegas. It included a private limousine, a personal chef, butler service, a patio large enough to have a party on, and a regular-size inground swimming pool.

The limousine picked her up at the airport. She'd arrived ahead of Giorgio and dismissed the butler. Maddie liked to unpack her own clothes and not rely on the hotel staff. She definitely wanted to hide the dress she'd bought for Valentine's Day from Giorgio. She had some other surprises planned for him as well.

It was late morning when Giorgio walked into the suite. He pulled her into his arms, sliding his big hands to her buttocks, and he pressed his hips against her. "I have missed you."

"I can feel how much." She smiled. "I missed you too."

His mouth swooped down on hers, and she lost herself in

his kiss. A heaviness settled at the apex of her legs, and she moaned against him.

"Where is your luggage?"

"I told the concierge I would call down when I wanted my bags delivered." Maddie smiled at that. Giorgio was as eager as she was to get into bed.

"Come with me… I have a surprise for you." She laced her fingers with his and pulled him along to the bedroom, past the turned-down king-size bed and into the bathroom. The tub was filled, and the jacuzzi swirling. Tall and short candles were lit and placed around the back ledge of the tub. She'd set the lighting from the crystal chandelier on low.

His arms wrapped around her waist, dragging her back into him. His sexy, husky voice breathed against her neck. "I see your cauldron is waiting,"

She turned in his arms. "Yes. I want to cast my spell over you."

His knuckles caressed her cheek. "Strega, you have already done that."

She pulled her blouse over her head, dropping it to the marble floor. Maddie unbuttoned his shirt and pushed it off his shoulders, running her hands over his pecs, stopping to rub her thumbs over his flat nipples before moving to his biceps. He tugged his arms from his sleeves. They'd been stripping each other while they spoke.

She kept her bra and panties on and said, "You get in. I want to… well, you'll see."

He pulled off his socks and stepped out of his boxers. His erection grew larger as she gazed at him. Giorgio eased into the tub and sat, resting his head on the rim. She picked up a bar of soap and made a fragrant lather between her hands, then she ran her palms over his shoulders and the broad expanse of his chest. She scraped her fingernail along his jaw.

"You shaved on the plane?"

"Yes, for you, strega." He pulled her to him, taking her lips in a gentle kiss before he said, "I showered too, but don't let that stop you."

"Good because I want to touch *all* of you." She reached around to lather his back then rinsed him before moving down to run her soapy hands under the water on his legs. His erection brushed her arm, sending heat into her core.

"As long as I can touch too."

While she soaped him, he played with her breasts. His fingers drew wet patterns over the cups of her bra and around her areola, exciting her nipple before moving onto the other. She held back a moan as her nipples stiffened, and an excited pulse beat between her legs.

Maddie swatted his hands away. "Come on; stand." She took a big, fluffy towel from the heated rack and started at his shoulders, drying his back. Then she dried the slight smattering of dark hair on his chest, following the thin line over his abs to his narrow hips.

She knelt and softly ran the towel over his erection before she kissed the smooth, velvety head. Maddie dried his muscular legs and feet. She left the towel on the floor and standing, she meshed her fingers with his and led him to the king-sized bed. She'd drawn the window coverings open so they could see the fabulous view of Las Vegas Boulevard from the bed. The dazzling neon lights never went out, even though it was mid-morning.

"Lie down on your stomach," she spoke in a soft whisper.

He did, and she slipped off her panties before straddling his back. Maddie reached to the nightstand for the fragrant massage oil she'd purchased on her Rodeo Drive shopping spree. Heating some in her palms, she slid her oiled hands up his broad back to his shoulders, kneading the muscles there and into his neck. Then down his tanned torso as her fingers traced the bulging muscles, she massaged his back and down his spine.

"Ahh," his husky, deep voice simmered with passion, "you have been keeping secrets."

She grinned. "What, this?"

She was thrilled that she'd thought to buy a book on intimate massage. Scooting down his body, she applied more oil to her palms and dug her fingers into the firm flesh of his buttock. She used the heel of her palm to apply pressure in circular motions, then she did the same to his other butt cheek before moving down the backs of his thighs. "You like it?" she asked.

Giorgio rolled over onto his back, pushing up to rest against the pillows. His aqua eyes burned with desire. His Italian accent heavy as he said, "See how much I like it." He held his erect flesh. "Come here, *strega*, and massage this." He dragged her up his legs and onto his thighs, spreading hers to straddle him.

Giorgio cupped her neck with one hand as their lips met. He touched her center, slipping a long, thick finger into her. "Oh, yes, wet and ready." Maddie moved on him, and he held her above his erection. He was at her entrance.

She pouted. "Oh, but I wanted to use my mouth."

He groaned. "I wouldn't last past your lips touching me."

He lowered her onto him. Her eyes closed at the pleasure. Giorgio unhooked her bra, skimming his hands on her shoulders, sliding the satin straps down her arms, and removing the bra. He kissed her breasts. Maddie eased herself down the length of his long, thick shaft, filling her. She held him in her body while he sucked on the stiff peak of her nipple, and his fingers played with her other breast.

Sucking her nipple into his mouth, his teeth held her as he tongued the bud. "Oh, yes, yes," she cried as his massive length stretched her and filled her.

Maddie moved on him, riding him faster and faster. Giorgio held her hips as he thrust up into her. A moan ripped through her as she climaxed in hot waves of pleasure. She fell forward on his chest, and he kissed her mouth while his hands skimmed from her hips up her back.

Her inner walls rippled around him as he held her in his arms. When her heartbeat slowed from racing, she pushed herself up from his chest, loving the way his huge maleness felt in her as she sat on him.

Giorgio pressed her clit with his finger, sending her into another orgasm. She loved this and the fire he had ignited in her burned while her vaginal muscles stroked him into her.

"Yes, *vita mia*, just like that." Her body held him, taking him deeper as he thrust up.

She gazed down at where they were joined, his dark hair mixed with her blonde curls. Maddie ran her hands over his taut abdominal muscles. "Ahh, *si*," he groaned, holding her hips down on him while he thrust two more times.

His face contorted with pleasure, his lips parted, and his shout vibrated through her as she felt the eruption and hot spurts of his orgasm filled her. They were covered in a sheen of passion. The musky scent of the massage oil lingered in the air. Maddie shook her head, and her hair fell around them. He was so handsome leaning against the pillows, she brushed his hair back from his brow.

Maddie leaned forward and placed her open palms on his cheeks. She kissed him, a long, lingering kiss, stroking her tongue on his. Twining her tongue around his, not giving him a chance to take over, she kissed his jaw and down his neck. Then she pushed up on him and looked into his aqua eyes. "I love you, Giorgio."

His brilliant smile melted her. He ran his hands along her back, then he turned her to lie on the bed. "Vita mia…" His knee parted her legs. "I have loved you forever," his husky voice whispered as he thrust into her. He raised her knees to his waist, moving in her again.

Maddie locked her ankles behind his back, holding onto his shoulders. She was so ready for him. Deep, long thrusts filled her over and over again and had her coming in a mind-shattering orgasm, and he came with her. He held his weight from her and then dragged her to his side.

"I love you more than my life," he said as he smoothed her hair from her brow and kissed her temple.

They slept until the late afternoon. Maddie woke first and lay in the circle of Giorgio's arms. She was content, and for the first time in a long time, Maddie accepted without any doubt that he did love her.

Giorgio's arms tightened around her, and she glanced at him. His eyes were closed, and his long lashes laid on his chiseled cheeks, a smile spread across his lips. "Was it a dream or did you say you love me?"

"It was definitely *not* a dream."

"Tell me again," he said, rolling over, pinning her to the mattress.

"I love you, Giorgio, with all my heart and soul."

Giorgio slipped on one of the hotel robes before he called down to the concierge to have his bags brought up. Maddie had unpacked a satin robe that she'd purchased on Rodeo Drive; it was powder blue and bordered in white satin, reaching mid-calf. She'd even bought a pair of sexy slippers.

While the butler unpacked Giorgio's clothes, Giorgio poured two drinks. Handing her one, they walked out to the penthouse suite's private patio and sat together on a double chaise lounge near their pool. Giorgio slid his arm around Maddie, pulling her in for a kiss. He placed a velvet jewelry box on her lap.

She looked into his aqua-blue eyes before she said, "Tomorrow's Valentine's Day."

"This is just because… I love you."

"Oh." She lifted the hinged lid. "Giorgio, it's beautiful," she said, taking the sapphire and diamond pendant from its resting place and holding it to her. She turned her back to Giorgio. "Can you fasten it?"

He brushed her long, blonde hair to the side before he did. Then she felt his lips on the back of her neck, and she leaned into his chest. Once the butler left, they went back into their suite, and Maddie admired the necklace in a mirror. "I love it; it's beautiful," she said, smiling at him. "I'm going to wear it to dinner tonight."

"*Vita mia*, you are the beauty. I love you."

They dressed and took their private limousine to watch the fountain show at the Bellagio and then dinner at an authentic Japanese restaurant in Las Vegas' very own China Town.

He'd surprised her when they'd ordered Japanese food in her apartment. He was an expert with chopsticks, unlike Doug who would embarrass her and play walrus. She and Giorgio drank sake, and both expertly used their chopsticks to enjoy the delicious entrée.

THEY RETURNED to their hotel late in the night. "I ordered a special Valentine's Day breakfast in bed for us. Complete with champagne and chocolate-filled *cornetti*."

"Oh, that sounds delicious. But not too early, right?"

He growled as he buried his lips against her neck. His beard tickled her as he said, "No, we can sleep in."

"Oh, sleep, is that what you think I want?"

Giorgio slid her zipper down the back of her raspberry-colored dress and then yanked the skimpy fabric from her. "I love your naked breasts," he said as he backed her up against the wall of windows in the living room.

She gasped, "Ohhh."

"Is that too cool against you? Don't worry, we're going to fog up the glass and warm you up."

"The window, people can see in," she said.

"No, the glass is one way. We have this magnificent view, but only I can see your naked body."

At his words, Maddie pulled his hips against her, and his knee spread her thighs. "Yes, then definitely warm me."

He tilted her chin back with his fingers. "I love you."

She gazed into his aqua eyes. "I love you too."

His mouth covered hers, coaxing her to open her lips to his. When she reached for his pants, he turned her and pressed her against the glass, leaning into her with one forearm across her breasts. His hand cupped the fullness as he played with a nipple between his callused thumb and finger.

"Oh, Giorgio, yes."

His other hand slipped down her belly, inching to her mound. She felt his erection through his pants, pressing into her buttock. She wiggled against him. Heat flooded her core, and she rested her forehead against the window.

Giorgio slid his hand back up her abdomen, and his lips lingered over the nape of her neck. She tried to touch him.

"Keep your hands on the window." His sexy Italian accent sent shivers up her spine.

She held in the moan. "I'm so ready… I… Ohh… ahh." She groaned when he nipped at her neck and plunged his finger into her. He played with her folds, reaching up to her clit and then plunging his finger into her again and again. "Giorgio…"

"Si, amore, come like this."

She groaned and shuddered. She arched her spine against him and on the next thrust, he used two long fingers, and that was all she needed. The waves of her orgasm held him in her, and Giorgio whispered into her ear, "I feel you so tight stroking my fingers… That's it, come for me."

Her knees buckled, and Giorgio turned her in his arms and lifted her so she could wrap her legs around him. He carried her into their bedroom. The covers had been turned down, and now he sat on the edge of the bed and lay back, pulling her over his chest. A delicious shudder ran through her.

"Giorgio, take your clothes off."

"Not yet." Heat sizzled through her veins at that. She reached for the top button of his shirt. "I can't be the only one naked." She laughed, and he rolled her onto her back.

"Strega, for what I have in mind, yes, you can."

IN THE MORNING, Maddie woke first. She was going to call and have their breakfast delivered, but Giorgio's arm snaked around her waist. "I have something for you." He snuggled against her back.

"Oh, yes… I feel that." She wiggled her backside closer to him, melting into his chest.

Smoothing her hair away from her face, he turned her head to reach her lips.

"I love waking up like this, surrounded by you," she said. She loved him, and she needed this.

He lifted her leg over his hip and pressed into her. "Ahh, yes. *Amore, per sempre.*" My love always.

They spent the morning in bed. They had a light lunch while sitting on the patio. Giorgio wanted to have an early dinner, and Maddie was happy with that. She brought a special dress to wear, and then he'd said maybe dancing *or* something else. He wouldn't elaborate on what the *something else* was. *Lots of sex,* she guessed.

After lunch, three staff members from the hotel's salon arrived in their suite. Maddie indulged in a massage and then hair, nails, the works.

When Giorgio stepped out for a few hours, she'd teased him, "You do know there are no vineyards here. It's desert." He laughed and said grapes weren't the only thing on his mind.

THE KNEE-LENGTH, blush-colored dress was exactly what she wanted. No red or other color associated with Valentine's Day. She wore her old crystal cherry blossom and silver sandals with the stiletto heel and a strap that wrapped around her ankle up to her lower calf. She asked Giorgio to fasten the blue sapphire necklace around her neck, and on her ears, she wore her diamond-stud earrings.

Valentine's Day dinner was elegant at Wynn's Costa Di Mare restaurant where each day, the chef had the seafood flown in from Italy. Giorgio ordered champagne, caviar, and one slice of decadent chocolate cake that they shared. All the symbols of love. She looked across their intimate table at the most handsome man in the restaurant—her date—her lover. His custom-made tuxedo accented broad shoulders and a very muscular body that she loved to run her hands over.

He smiled at her, and she melted into his gaze. So much had happened since they first met. Without realizing it, she went from casual sex to exclusivity. She was going back to Sicily with him to stay at his villa for a while. He wanted her to meet his mother someday soon. She was living at the Napa Vineyard. Overseeing the renovation of the mansion, transforming it into an intimate hotel and wedding venue.

He held her hand across the table. "I would like you to meet my mother one day." She squeezed his hand, not willing to commit to meeting his family.

They left the restaurant and took the limousine back to their hotel. Once off the elevator, they strolled down the plush-carpeted corridor to their suite. He closed the door and turned the lock. Giorgio held her to him, placing a soft kiss on her temple. His sexy scent filled her head; she would never get tired of this man. He reached into his pocket, taking a box out that she could see was a ring box. Maddie's heart skipped a fearful beat. Her eyes met his.

"Giorgio—"

"No, please. Don't say anything."

"Tell me it *is… not…* a diamond ring."

He opened the lid. Maddie tugged on a corner of her bottom lip. Giorgio tipped his head to one side and shrugged a tuxedo-covered shoulder as he said, "Pink… diamond. Does that count?"

Her lids slipped over her eyes. Her heart thudded. Then she looked at a pink, heart-shaped center stone surrounded by clear pear-shaped diamonds set at an angle around the center stone.

"Maddalena, this can be whatever you want it to be," his sexy voice whispered.

She brushed a tear from her cheek before gazing into his eyes. "Clearly, it's an engagement ring." She turned away, whispering, "I'm… so… confused."

"Let's not discuss this anymore… You know my feelings. I will wait for you." Giorgio came closer to her and brushed a kiss on her temple. "Why don't you choose the hand you want to wear my ring on?" A heartbeat later, he whispered in his husky Italian accent, "Choose your left hand."

She gazed into his aqua eyes, the compassion, love, and understanding drawing her. She loved him and had to trust Giorgio not to hurt her. She *loved* him. Oh, yes, she did. Their time in France had proved that to her. Their love was so much more than what she'd thought love was. Her heart hammered, bursting with passion for this man. Very slowly, she reached her left hand out to him, her fingers trembled.

He flashed one of his brilliant, intoxicating smiles—the one that transformed his face, making him more handsome —if that were possible—and blew her a kiss. Never taking his eyes from hers, he took the ring from the velvet box. Dropping the box to the floor, Giorgio, the man she loved, went down on one knee. "Marry me. Share my life. *You* are my life." He slid the ring on her finger. "I'm taking this as a yes."

As tears ran down her cheeks, she laughed. "Yes. Yes, you stubborn man. I will marry you. I love you, my very own winemaker."

"I love you, *vita mia*." Giorgio stood and bent to kiss her. Maddie looped her arms around his neck as he took her mouth with the gentlest sweeps of his sculpted lips, making her feel fragile.

She breathed against his lips. "Oh Giorgio, I do love you."

He dipped slightly and hooked his arm under her knees, lifting her against his chest, then he walked to the door.

"Where are we going? The bedroom is the other way."

He kissed her cheek. "We will get to the bedroom, but first, I have a surprise for you."

"More than this?" She held out her hand, admiring the beautiful ring that reminded her of a fairytale. "It fits perfectly."

Giorgio nuzzled her neck and carried her from their suite and down the hall. "I hope you'll like my surprise." In the elevator, he removed his arm from under her knees, and she stood. Giorgio pressed the button to the banquet floor.

"What are you up to?" she said with suspicion in her voice.

He shrugged a broad shoulder. "We're in Las Vegas so… Let's get married."

She gasped. "Right now? Oh Giorgio, yes. Yes. Is that

where you went earlier? Just you and me on Valentine's Day, yes."

He kissed her hand. "Don't be too angry with me," he said as he intertwined his fingers with hers. The elevator doors silently opened. Maddie frowned at him, but he took her hand in his and walked off the elevator and into the chapel receiving room. The director approached.

"Mr. Lombardo, welcome. All is at the ready."

A woman followed. "Hello, Miss Watson, and best wishes," she said. "I am your wedding attendant. Come with me please. Mr. Lombardo ordered flowers and a hair ornament for the pictures."

Maddie looked at Giorgio. "Pictures?"

"Why, of course, Miss Watson," the director said, then he turned to Giorgio. "Mr. Lombardo, follow me, please."

She looked at Giorgio, and he came to stand in front of her. He brushed his knuckles along her cheek, his gaze full of love. His strong arms held her for a moment. Then he whispered into her ear, "I'll be waiting for you at the front of the chapel. Don't be too long. *Vita mia... Ti amo.*"

Only Maddie knew what he did as he ran the tip of his tongue over the shell of her ear, and then he kissed her cheek. A shiver raced up her spine, and she melted at that. In a breathy whisper, she said, "Okay, I love you too."

The wedding attendant led Maddie into a dressing room. Piano music played through the speakers. A rose-colored velvet couch sat against one wall. On both sides of the couch were highly polished wooden end tables, each holding a vase of fresh flowers. Directly in front of the couch was a coffee table and on it, a tray with crystal glasses and an assortment of beverages.

The focus of the room was a large vanity with a tufted gold-velvet, low bench in front. The mirror was framed with lightbulbs lit to give off a soft glow. On top of the table laid a bouquet of pink and white roses.

"Mr. Lombardo picked these for you to carry down the aisle," the attendant said.

Maddie checked her makeup. Her cheeks were flushed with excitement, and then she applied the slightest touch of lip gloss. A knock on the door startled her.

The attendant said, "Everyone is waiting for you."

"Everyone?" Maddie asked just as the woman opened the door.

"Dad!" Maddie gasped.

"You look beautiful, sweetie."

"But how?"

"We're so happy for you. Giorgio called last week and flew in to see us, so that your mother and I could meet him. He explained his plan to us—your mom and I couldn't be

happier. I understand you may require something borrowed?"

"What? Oh!" Her fingers touched the blue sapphire necklace Giorgio had given her the day before. Now his earlier questions and comments became clear. "Is that a new dress? Are you wearing your old crystal sandals? I'm glad I chose this blue sapphire for you." *He'd planned this so well. He'd flown in unexpectedly last week... Now, in the elevator, he'd said, don't be too mad at me. How could I be angry? He knows my heart better than I do.*

"Mom thought you can borrow her bracelet." Her father helped Maddie fasten her mother's diamond tennis bracelet to her wrist. Last week, Giorgio had surprised her by coming in for a day on his way to Napa. So, he'd gone to her parents. She loved him so much.

Her father slipped her arm through the crook of his elbow and patted her hand. They walked to the chapel doors. "Are you ready?"

Her heart beat with joy and when the chapel doors opened, the wedding march began. She saw her mother, her brother, her sister-in-law, and niece, and a beautiful woman wearing a lavender dress with pitch-black hair curling around her shoulders stood near Giorgio.

"That's Giorgio's mother Angela," Maddie's dad whispered.

These were the only people who mattered. Then she looked at the man standing with the officiant. Giorgio, the love of her life, waited for her as she stepped into her future

Thank you for reading The Winemaker's Seduction. I hope you enjoyed Maddie and Giorgio's love story.

The Frenchman's Revenge is the next book in the DiMarco Empire Series.

Enter a world where one ruthless woman, Angela DiMarco Lombardo and one pleasure seeking billionaire Andre Bourbon blur the lines between lust and love. Decency and Revenge.

Andre Bourbon is enraged when he learns how thoroughly deceived he was by Angela and how she used him. Playing him for a fool in more ways than one. He is consumed with rage. Kidnapping her from her home in Palermo and holding her captive in his Paris mansion is just the beginning. His blinding rage demands that he must possess the Sicilian beauty. He won't rest until he owns her body, mind, and soul.

Grab The Frenchman's Revenge an Enemies to Lovers, Reverse Age Play Romance

<u>The Frenchman's Revenge</u>

WHERE TO FIND MY BOOKS

You can find my books at your favorite bookstore, retailer, or library

Or, you can buy them directly from me at my website https:// CindyReddingAuthor.com

Or,

Cindy's Store https://payhip.com/CindyRedding

If you prefer, please scan this QR code with your phone.

ALSO BY CINDY REDDING

The DiMarco Empire Series

The Sicilian's Betrayal

The Winemaker's Seduction

<u>The Frenchman's Revenge</u>

<u>The Sea Captains Redemption</u>

Christmas

A Fake Date For Kate

The Christmas Present

The Royals

A Royal Temptation

More Romances

The Tycoon's Secret Child

ABOUT THE AUTHOR

USA TODAY Bestselling Author **Cindy Redding** writes what she loves. Contemporary sizzling romance. Inspired by her travels around the world and her love of Italy, Cindy's romances come alive with hot-blooded men and strong-willed independent women. Escape to a world where happily ever after lives.

https://www.cindyreddingauthor.com

ACKNOWLEDGMENTS

I am fortunate enough to have not one, but two editors.

I would like to thank Heather Starling for all of her invaluable advice and wonderful insight. Thank you for listening to me rant during this crazy 2020.

I want to especially thank SJS Editorial Services for their quick and thorough editing. You make me shine.

9 781735 550534